"You are going to wear a veil, aren't you, Deborah?"

Aunt Ida went on anxiously, "You *are* eligible for one, aren't you?"

Deborah lost power of speech. The idea of Aunt Ida matter-of-factly inquiring if she were still a virgin and therefore entitled to the symbolic veil....

Behind her, a husky voice said, "Of course, she's going to wear a veil. I have dreams about Debbie in a veil." Riley's arms went around her in an enthusiastic bear hug.

Ida's look of concern faded into something like genuine amusement. "What a lucky girl you are, dear," she murmured.

Riley pressed his lips to the side of her throat. "Yes, you are," he whispered. "A very lucky girl that I came along just in time to stop that kind of question."

They were halfway down the hill when Riley asked casually, "By the way, can you wear a veil?"

Deborah's voice was pure ice. "What possible business is it of yours?"

Leigh Michaels likes to write warm, family-oriented stories set in Midwestern cities or small towns. A midwesterner from birth, she now lives in Ottumwa, Iowa, in a house that she toured with her real-estate agents seven times in twelve months. The first six times, she told them she hated it. The seventh time, she bought it. Now, whenever she isn't in her big, sunny office helping her characters live happily ever after, she's apt to be out in the acre of grounds—flower gardens, controlled woodlands and rolling lawn—that she has ruefully named The Garden of Weedin'.

Books by Leigh Michaels

HARLEQUIN ROMANCE
3010—NO PLACE LIKE HOME
3023—LET ME COUNT THE WAYS
3070—A MATTER OF PRINCIPAL
3086—AN IMPERFECT LOVE
3119—AN UNCOMMON AFFAIR
3141—PROMISE ME TOMORROW

HARLEQUIN PRESENTS
1107—CLOSE COLLABORATION
1147—A NEW DESIRE
1245—ONCE AND FOR ALWAYS
1266—WITH NO RESERVATIONS

TEMPORARY MEASURES

Leigh Michaels

Harlequin Books

TORONTO • NEW YORK • LONDON
AMSTERDAM • PARIS • SYDNEY • HAMBURG
STOCKHOLM • ATHENS • TOKYO • MILAN

ISBN 0-373-03160-2

Harlequin Romance first edition November 1991

TEMPORARY MEASURES

CHAPTER ONE

CHICAGO'S MAGNIFICENT Mile—the mad bustle of pedestrians surging in waves down the sidewalks, the constant roar of traffic on North Michigan Avenue, the distant
wail of a dozen sirens scurrying in all directions—she had
missed it all.

Coming home to Chicago was by far the best part of her
frequent business trips, Deborah Ainsley thought as she
made her way with the ease of long practice through the
rivers of people on the sidewalk until she reached the safe
haven of a small sheltered entry. She stopped just inside the
glass door of the Ainsley Gallery and swung the canvas bag
down from her shoulder, reaching into it for a pair of ul-
trafashionable high-heeled pumps to replace the running
shoes that had smoothed her walk along the Magnificent
Mile from her apartment not far from the lakeshore. She
dropped the running shoes into the bag, straightened the
paisley scarf at her throat—the only bright accent against
her cream-colored dress—and stopped to admire a tiny oil
painting that glowed like a jewel against a gray velvet drape
on an easel near the entrance.

The gallery was quiet and peaceful, a haven that en-
couraged the art lover to browse and study and meditate as
he would in a library or in a museum or in a church. It was
almost dim, except where subtle, spot-lighting empha-
sized a painting here and there, inviting the observer to
look deeply and fall in love.

The Ainsley Gallery was not large, but in the three years since it opened, Deborah had carved out a niche among the hundreds of galleries in the Chicago metropolitan area; she had gained a reputation for handling the best new contemporary artists in the region. If a client wanted a Dali print or a Monet poster, the Ainsley Gallery politely suggested a competitor who specialized in those things. But for the Chicagoan who wanted to own an original piece of art instead of a mass-produced copy, but who couldn't afford the tremendous prices of already well-known artists, the Ainsley Gallery was the best place to go.

The art of tomorrow, Deborah called it. After all, as she had frequently been heard to say, a majority of the paintings hanging in the Art Institute of Chicago had not cost millions—they had been purchased originally by ordinary people, with ordinary pocket money, simply because they were attractive, and only in later years had the judgment of the art world made them valuable. And, she was fond of saying, it would inevitably happen again, with some of the very paintings her clients were buying now.

Already, several of the artists whose work Deborah had hung in her early shows had gained a national reputation. That was why she kept seeking out new ones whose work was still affordable to the secretary with a walk-up apartment, or to the couple furnishing their first house in the suburbs. That was why she had been in Michigan all week, and that was why she was so delighted to be home once more.

She ran a practiced eye around the gallery, not even trying to look at each piece, but instead observing the symmetry and grace of how things were hung, how the placement of paintings and sculpture invited the client to wander and observe. Peggy deserved a compliment, she decided; she was by far the best assistant Deborah had ever had.

A classical melody rippled from the speakers concealed in the walls, playing so softly that it scarcely broke the surface of her conscious mind. It did not drown out the sound of the discreet doorbell, or of the low-voiced conversation at the back of the gallery, where Peggy was telling a client about the person who had created the luscious watercolor he was admiring.

Deborah turned with a professional smile, to greet the customer who had just come in. Then her expression warmed into a delighted glow, and she hurried toward the gray-haired man who had stopped to admire the same tiny oil that had caught her eye as she came in. She slipped a hand into the crook of his elbow. "It's wonderful, isn't it, Daddy? Peggy was absolutely right to put it there, where it catches everyone's eye—"

William Ainsley gave her a wry half smile. "Do you ever take your mind off art, Deborah?"

"Oh—I haven't seen you in two weeks, have I?" She darted a coquettish look up at him. "I *am* sorry not to have shown you how happy I am to see you. Of course, it's not my fault that you haven't changed an iota in ten years. When a man simply stays as handsome as you are—"

"Watch out," he warned. "You're sailing a bit close to the shoals."

Deborah grinned and leaned her head against his shoulder. Her long, glossy brown hair swung smoothly against his gray linen jacket. "You're right," she admitted. "The truth is, when a man stays as handsome as you are, everybody notices. I was just too bowled over for words when you walked in."

"Rubbish. How much are you asking for that painting, Deborah?"

She glanced at the discreet tag on the velvet next to the gold frame. "Nine hundred. But for you, Daddy, I could make a special deal."

"And sell it to me for a thousand, I suppose." He looked at it again. "I should stay out of here. You know my weaknesses too well when it comes to buying paintings." He turned his back on the easel with determination.

Deborah smothered a smile. "You're the one who dragged me to the museums every Saturday," she pointed out. "And to the galleries after school, and to the art fairs on Sundays."

"I should get a special deal, that's for sure," William Ainsley said a bit grumpily. "You'll inherit my entire collection and have it all back again someday, anyway."

"Not for a very long time, I hope."

He pretended to misunderstand. "Yes, and I suppose you'll make an even larger profit when you sell it the second time. Well, beware—if you do, I'll haunt the damned gallery."

"Oh, good," Deborah murmured. "My very own ghost. It'll be a marvelous advertising gimmick." She looked up at him through long black lashes.

"Humph." But there was a sparkle in his eyes, and she couldn't help laughing in response.

"So why are you here?" she asked. "I don't often see you on Wednesday mornings, you know."

"I thought perhaps we'd have dinner at my club tonight."

"Oh, I can't. Bristol's leaving town tomorrow on a business trip, and we're going to Coq au Vin tonight." She saw his face fall, and regretted having to refuse him; he'd been so lonely in the past few years since her mother died, and though she tried to spend time with him, she was so busy and out of town so much that it was difficult. He was also far too sensitive about intruding on her life, she thought, and sometimes when she had to refuse an invitation it was weeks before he asked again. "Why don't you join us?" she said.

"Oh, no. I'm sure Bristol will want you to himself."

She laughed. "He won't mind. Bristol's an adult, after all—too mature to be jealous."

"That's for certain."

It was only a murmur, almost under his breath, and for an instant Deborah wasn't quite sure she'd heard properly.

Then William sighed and said, "Your mother would probably be stepping on my toes by now to shut me up, I'm sure, but I feel I have to say it anyway. Deborah, I wish you weren't seeing quite so much of Bristol."

"I thought you liked him."

"I respect him," William corrected.

"Isn't that what I said? He's the foundation's attorney, after all. You hired him, and you introduced him to me—"

"I introduce you to nearly everybody who works for the foundation, Deborah, but that doesn't mean I want you to start dating them all. Dammit, honey, the man is old enough to be your father."

"I beg your pardon," Deborah said crisply, "but fourteen years' age difference does not exactly make him old enough to be my father!"

"Well, he certainly acts like an antique," William Ainsley muttered. "You aren't thinking of marrying him, are you?"

After a long moment Deborah said quietly, "I simply enjoy his company, Daddy. Shall we just leave it at that?"

William stared at his black wing tips and drew a pattern on the carpet with the toe of one of them. "I understand, of course. After the experience you had with that artist, the security that Bristol represents must look very—"

"Daddy, shall we leave it?" she repeated. It was very soft.

He stopped drawing lines on the carpet and looked at her with sad-puppy eyes. "You sound just like your mother," he said. "Vivien could have stopped an army division with that tone of voice."

Deborah's eyes misted. Her mother was never far from her mind, and the longing loneliness in William's voice could have melted glass. It turned Deborah's heart, always a bit soft where her father was concerned, into a soggy puddle.

"I'm sorry, darling," he said unsteadily. "Of course it's your business. But I'm so worried about you. All I want for you is what your mother and I had."

"Oh, is that all?" Deborah asked a bit wryly. "That's a tall order, Daddy." She hugged him tightly, her head buried against his shoulder, her nose tickled by the spicy scent of his after-shave lotion. "How about tomorrow?" she whispered. "I'll even buy your dinner."

He smiled. "It's a date, honey." He kissed her cheek and gently set her aside. "I suppose I should let you get to work, shouldn't I?"

"I'd better. After a week away, my desk probably doesn't bear thinking about." As he put a hand on the doorknob, she called, "Oh, Daddy..." He turned, and she added impishly, with a gesture toward the easel, "Shall I have the painting delivered?"

William Ainsley's eyebrows climbed. "Of course," he said, as if there had never been any doubt. "Why do you think I came in, anyway?" Then he winked and ducked out into the maelstrom of North Michigan Avenue before she could retort.

SHE WAS WRITING notes of thanks to the clients and artists she had visited in Michigan when Peggy came into their shared office and dropped into the chair beside Deborah's desk. "He bought the watercolor," she said. "Patience pays off again."

"I seem to remember telling you that if a person doesn't buy something on his first visit, it doesn't mean he won't ever make a purchase at all."

"I know. 'A client who does not buy is not a lost sale, but an opportunity,'" Peggy recited. "But he's been an opportunity three times a week for the past month, and I was starting to think he was only coming in to stare at my age spots."

Deborah didn't look up from the jade green envelope she was addressing. "They're freckles," she corrected mildly.

"Yes, but I'm sure he wouldn't agree. When one hits forty-five, you know..." Peggy reached into her top desk drawer for a tiny mirror and studied herself in it. "I'm so terribly average," she said dispassionately. "Not short, not tall. Not fat, but certainly not slender. My hair can't even make up its mind whether to be blond or brown. It's unfair that my sole distinguishing feature is freckles. I should have outgrown them in my teens." The doorbell chimed and she put away the mirror and went out to greet the new client. Then she leaned back into the office to say, "I forgot—it's in your messages, but I said I'd make sure to tell you anyway. Your cousin is awfully anxious to talk to you. Riley—is that his name?"

Deborah sealed the envelope and reached for another one. "That's his name, all right."

"He sounded like the sort of man who might appreciate freckles."

Deborah spread a sheet of engraved notepaper on her blotter. "I should hope so," she said. "He certainly has plenty of them himself. But sounds can be deceiving. Especially when it's Riley who's making the noise."

She finished writing her notes and stacked them, stamped and ready to go, on the corner of her desk before she even bothered to look through the stack of messages. But her conscience had started to nag at her long before that. It was hardly fair to assume Riley was still behaving like the annoying teenager who had seemed to find his greatest pleasure in tormenting the life out of her. After all, she hadn't seen him in years. He must be thirty by now.

"Thirty-one," she muttered. "He's three years older than you, Deborah, and as much as you hate to admit it, you're going to be twenty-eight soon."

She found the pink message slip midway down in the pile. It was crammed with tiny, cramped writing, and on closer examination she discovered it wasn't a single lengthy message but a record of nearly a dozen calls made over the past three days. Peggy was right, she thought idly. Riley *was* awfully anxious to talk to her.

The number listed was a Chicago one, and she was mildly surprised when it was answered by the switchboard at the Englin Hotel, which efficiently put her through to Riley's room.

He must have come up for a few days of rest and recreation in the city, she thought, *and he probably wants someone to take him to the zoo or something. Not a bad idea. He'd be right at home there with the rest of the animals....*

"Yankee Stadium, home plate umpire speaking," said a voice in her ear.

She wanted to groan. Hadn't the man even started to grow up? "Shall I call back after the game's over?" she asked tartly.

The voice warmed. "Debbie darling! I'm glad to see the natives didn't get restless in Michigan and do something nasty to you."

"Peggy actually told you that's where I was?"

"Only in self-defense, I assure you. She'd never have breathed a word if it hadn't been me asking."

"I certainly have no trouble in believing that," Deborah said dryly. "What brings you to the Windy City, Riley?"

"Research," he said promptly.

And that, she thought helplessly, gave her precisely no information at all.

"And since I'm here, I thought I'd take you out to dinner and bring you up-to-date on all the family gossip."

"What now? Has Mary Beth run off with the mailman or something?"

"Of course not," he said with offended dignity, and then ruined the effect by adding candidly, "my esteemed sister has gained twenty pounds since her new baby came along—"

"Another baby? No one told me."

"Well, it's not exactly a *new* baby. I mean the one that's almost four now. At any rate, the mailman probably wouldn't have her. He's rather a handsome guy."

"Oh? Do you find yourself attracted to good-looking men these days?"

"Not at all." Riley sounded wounded. "I didn't notice it myself. Mom told me that he's one good-looking fellow. How's tonight? For dinner, I mean."

"I assumed that was what you meant." It was cool. "I can't. I have a dinner date."

He didn't seem offended. "Oh? Are you still dating the thing with the beard that you brought to your Uncle Ralph's funeral?"

"Why do you want to know?" The tone was a little more crisp than Deborah had intended.

Riley didn't seem to notice. "So I can tell Mary Beth the gory details, of course."

"I didn't even know you were at Uncle Ralph's funeral."

"I came late and left early. You didn't exactly stay long in the bosom of the family, yourself."

"Morgan didn't—" She stopped. It was certainly none of Riley's business.

"Morgan? What a name. How about tomorrow night?"

"No. I have a—"

"Dinner date. I'm amazed," Riley mused. "I didn't think that something like that would bother to comb the crumbs out of his facial fur in order to go out two days in a row."

Deborah was doing a slow simmer. "If you're finished, Riley—"

"Deb! Darling Debbie, don't hang up on me. I'm sorry I made noises about your fuzzy friend. Is that honestly his first name, or did he choose it as a protest statement? Never mind. I won't do it again, honest. I really do need to talk to you."

"Family gossip," she muttered. "I suppose next you're going to tell me Aunt Ida's fallen in love!"

"How did you guess?"

There was a long silence. Finally Deborah said, "You're not going to say any more, are you? Well, since etiquette obliges me not to be rude to family—"

"Wonderful thing, etiquette. I've always believed in it."

She didn't bother to counter that one. "I can arrange to be free the day after tomorrow."

"That's Friday." She could almost hear him shaking his head. "I have to go home Friday. How about breakfast tomorrow?"

"Civilized people don't eat breakfast, Riley. All right, all right. I have to admit I'm dying to find out what sort of tall tale you can concoct about Aunt Ida."

"No tall tales. I outgrew that years ago."

"Right," she said. "And I suppose you really are a home plate umpire at Yankee Stadium, too."

IF RILEY'S GOAL was to intrigue her, Deborah had to admit he'd succeeded; she didn't even remember eating her vichyssoise at Coq au Vin that night. In fact, as they were finishing their quail Normandy, Bristol said with heavy politeness, "Do pardon me if I'm boring you by talking about my business conference, Deborah."

"What? No, not at all. I've scarcely heard a word—" She choked back the rest of that sentence and said, "I'm sorry, Bristol. I was thinking about my cousin, you see."

Bristol Wellington waited until the wine steward had refilled his glass and then said punctiliously, "Your cousin? I thought neither of your parents had siblings."

"Oh, not my first cousin. He's... I'm not even sure what, it's so distant. My great-grandfather and his great-grandfather were brothers."

Bristol looked faintly interested. "Then the two of you are third cousins," he announced.

"Thank you," Deborah said politely. "I never could figure these things out. He's in town, and I'm going to have breakfast with him tomorrow."

"One should always maintain cordial relationships with one's family," Bristol murmured. "I, myself, correspond with—"

"That's easy to say. Of course, with Riley—"

"Riley?" Bristol sounded as if he'd bitten into something sour.

"Riley Lassiter," Deborah added helpfully. "He is from one branch of the Lassiter family, my mother was from the other. His branch got to keep the ancestral name, but her branch got most of the money. It always seemed like a fair trade to me. You see, what actually happened is that the original Lassiter brothers—the great-grandfathers I was telling you about—had a falling-out, and Riley's ancestor sold out to mine for a mere pittance, right before the patents they held became valuable."

"And I suppose he holds a grudge."

"Riley? I don't think he has a grudging bone in his body."

Bristol asked suspiciously, "He isn't a criminal element or the like, is he?"

"Who knows, with Riley." She sipped her wine. "You know, it's almost embarrassing, but I honestly don't know what Riley does. His parents had a farm near Summerset in southern Illinois, where the Lassiters all started out. Riley was just ready to begin law school when his father died. I know he dropped out of school, but I haven't any idea what he did instead, or what he's doing now."

"Raising pigs, probably," Bristol said. "Really, Deborah, must we—"

"It's a shame," she mused. "Mother always kept up with these things. I'll bet she even knew the names and birthdays of all of Mary Beth's kids...." There was a catch in her voice that surprised her.

Bristol sighed. He didn't ask who Mary Beth was.

"When I was a kid, I spent a lot of time down there, too," Deborah said. "I thought that Mother sent me down every summer just to get rid of me. Now I'm sure it was because she wanted me to have a close relationship with the little family that's left, Aunt Ida and Uncle Ralph and Riley's parents. Actually, it's too bad that it didn't work out that way." She stopped abruptly. "I'm sorry, Bristol. I didn't mean to bore you to extinction."

He bowed his head. "You could never do that, Deborah. I must confess, however, that I fail to see why—"

"Why I'm fixed on Riley tonight?" She stopped. She hadn't exactly thought about it herself till right now. "I suppose it's just that the whole thing is rather strange...his calling me," she said slowly. "I mean, he must have been in Chicago now and then, but I've never heard a word from him before. Now, suddenly..."

Aunt Ida's fallen in love, she had said. And Riley had answered, *How did you guess?*

No, she thought uneasily. He couldn't possibly be serious. Riley never was.

HE HAD ASKED HER to meet him in the hotel lobby. She was still yawning as she paid off her cab and stepped through gleaming brass revolving doors into the huge reception hall of the Englin Hotel, one of the city's grandest and oldest. But her sleepiness disappeared with a bang as she stopped short under a silver and crystal chandelier that was the size of the average automobile. "Damn," she muttered under her breath. "I forgot this place has about fifteen lobbies." Where, she wondered, was Riley likely to be waiting?

"Right here," a voice murmured behind her, as if he'd read her mind, and she wheeled around to face...Riley? she thought in disbelief. *This* was the same person as the gangly teenager with the red hair and the freckles and the ears that seemed too large for his head?

He smiled, and she relaxed a little. Yes, this was Riley, all right. Riley of the dancing hazel eyes and the perpetually mischievous grin. But what had happened to the rest of him?

Well, the hair still had a reddish cast; it was actually a rather wonderful shade of burnished auburn now. But the freckles were gone, and the gangly body was now well-knit and very athletic looking in a trimly tailored pin-striped shirt and dark trousers. No tie, no jacket, but then what had she expected of Riley?

"You finally grew into your ears," she said.

He kissed her cheek lightly. "And you're looking very well, too, Debbie darling," he murmured. "Much better than you did at Ralph's funeral. You were so pale then that I wondered for a while which one of you was the corpse."

Deborah sighed. "I knew it was too good to last."

"You're the one who brought up ears," he chided.

"I'll remember that it's a sensitive spot." She reached up and tugged gently at his earlobe. "It is good to see you, Riley."

He tucked her hand into the crook of his elbow and took her across the lobby to the Captain's Table, where a smiling waiter showed them to a table and poured their coffee.

"Honestly, you didn't have to make up tales about Aunt Ida to get me to come to breakfast, you know," Deborah went on. "I don't hold it against you anymore that you were a terror when you were a kid."

His eyes started to sparkle. "Remember the time out on the farm when you were having a tea party for your dolls and I put the frog in the teapot?"

"Do I remember! When I lifted the lid and he leaped out at me—"

"I haven't heard such a shriek since. It's a good thing it was only pretend tea," Riley mused. "If you'd managed the real thing, we would all have been in hot water."

Deborah groaned. "Especially the poor frog."

"And you've forgiven me for all that?" He looked somber and serious; Deborah was morally certain that it was only a momentary lapse.

"Certainly. Besides," she added gently, "you can't possibly put a frog in my cup at breakfast. This is the Englin Hotel, after all."

"Do you honestly think that would stop me?" It was very soft.

She looked at her cup, suddenly suspicious.

He laughed. "No, Debbie, I've outgrown that sort of thing long ago."

"I suppose I'll have to take your word for it. How is your mother, by the way?"

"Happy as a clam. She's remarried, you know. Or didn't you?"

Deborah's forehead furrowed. "I think Daddy mentioned it, yes. She must have sent him a Christmas card or something."

"She and her new husband have turned the farm into a gigantic truck garden—everything from cabbages to kings, you might say."

"You're not still on the farm yourself then?" The waiter brought their plates. She eyed Riley's platter-size Denver omelet with a jaundiced expression. "Someone ought to tell you about cholesterol," she murmured, as she broke an oatmeal muffin in half.

He cut into the omelet and gave her a soulful look. "Deb darling, I didn't know you cared."

The nickname was beginning to grate a bit, but she had no trouble remembering what had happened the last time she had instructed him that her name was Deborah. She'd been almost eleven then and very serious about the fact that she was not Deb or Debbie. Riley had listened, patiently and perfectly straight-faced, and from then on he had called her Deborah, as she had requested. The problem was that he put the accent on the second syllable, and slurred it a little, until it sounded like a native of Brooklyn referring to a tiresome pest—da bore.

Deb darling, she concluded, however insincere it might be, was certainly an improvement over that!

"Besides," Riley said without looking up, "I know all about cholesterol. I'm running a restaurant now."

The statement was blithe, but underneath it she heard... what? Resentment? Self-pity? A sense of shame that the promising law student had come down to this?

She put down her muffin. "Oh, Riley—I'm so sorry," she said, and then wanted to bite her tongue off. As if he wanted her sympathy...as if it could do anything but make him feel worse!

He darted a curious glance at her; Deborah knew it, even though she was studying the china pattern, too embarrassed to look at him. "I'm—I shouldn't have said that," she muttered.

"Well, we can't all be dashing over the countryside discovering artists, can we?" he said reasonably. "Some of us wouldn't know one if we tripped over him. Me, for instance. As soon as I saw that bearded creature you had on a leash at Ralph's funeral, I said, there's an artist if I ever saw one. But for all I know he really spends his nights as a guard at the hospital for the criminally insane."

"He was an artist," she said reluctantly.

"*Was?* Does that mean he's stopped, or that he doesn't figure large in your life these days?"

Deborah's temper snapped. "Uncle Ralph's been dead for three years, Riley. For all you know, I could be working my way through every man in the Chicago telephone directory by now. So what business is it of yours whether I'm still seeing Morgan?"

He looked very innocent. "None at all," he said gently. "But if you'd like to talk about this sexual compulsion of yours, Deb—"

She bit her lip, knowing that once more she had reacted precisely as he had hoped she would.

He relented. "Sorry," he said briskly. "I don't see you as a nymphomaniac, actually, but I couldn't resist the impulse to see your expression. You really must learn to control that tendency of yours to make grandstand statements, you know."

"The only thing I need to control," Deborah said with commendable restraint, "is the amount of time I spend with you. And that will be very easy to do."

He shook his head. "I hope you'll think it over very seriously before you walk out of here, Deb."

"Why on earth should I?"

"Because we haven't even gotten to the problem of Aunt Ida yet."

"And her supposed lover? Oh, for heaven's sake, Riley, Ida's eighty if she's a day and she's been a spinster all her life."

"That's partly why I'm so worried." He actually sounded serious. "She must be infatuated or she wouldn't be acting like such an idiot."

Deborah stared at him for a long moment. "I suppose you're going to tell me she's acquired a gigolo! You can't expect me to take that notion seriously."

He was shaking his head. "Not a gigolo, exactly. He acts more like a tame python. Actually, he's a venture-capital specialist who wants to revive Paradise Valley."

"The bankrupt resort complex? It's been sitting there rotting for ten years. I can't believe Ida would give him a minute, much less any money...." Her voice wavered. "She hasn't, has she?"

"Ida is in it up to the crook of her Roman nose," Riley said. "For one thing, her suave new investment counselor is living at Lassiter House these days. And she's seriously considering investing not only her own money in his scam, but the trust's as well."

"The trust?" Deborah said weakly.

He nodded. "The trust. The unbreakable one that your great-grandfather wrote to protect his assets for his descendants—which is to say, you—yea, verily and unto the umpteenth generation. *That* trust."

"But what—"

"You see, he overlooked one weak spot. He put his kids in charge of the money—a sort of balance-of-power arrangement—but after Ralph died, your Aunt Ida was left as the sole trustee." He set down his cup with a firm click. "And now, Debbie darling, Ida can do any damned thing she wants with the cash."

CHAPTER TWO

"AND DON'T YOU DARE tell me it's only money," Riley went on. "I don't know anyone who's noble enough to whistle away the income on a few million dollars."

"Daddy does every year," she said only half-consciously.

"That's different. It's not his own cash, it belongs to the foundation, and it all goes to charmingly worthy causes. It's not the same thing at all when it's going to support a con man in the style to which he'd like to become accustomed."

"You're quite sure it's a scam?"

"Paradise Valley?" It was almost a shriek. "It isn't honestly a lake in the middle of that resort at all, you know. It's an industrial-size sink, Deb, and it has sucked more money down the drain . . ."

"You sound like a person who's lost a little cash in it yourself."

"Not me, but my father took a flier on it the first time around." He sounded grim. "Mother just finished paying off *that* mortgage on the farm last year."

"Oh. I see."

"No, I don't think you do. I forgot that you haven't been around Summerset for years, so of course you don't understand what's going on. Let me tell you, Paradise Valley will never be a successful vacation resort, because not enough people want to spend their time and money in

Summerset. It's not exactly the entertainment center of the world, you know. To draw the kind of crowd you'd need to make it pay would require a fantastic investment in a year-round amusement park, ski slopes and snowmobile trails as well as golf courses and tennis courts and beaches. To say nothing of the facilities to house all of them. It quickly reaches a point of diminishing returns—the more money you spend, the more people you have to accommodate, in a limited space, to earn it all back. The fact is, it can't be done."

"All right, so it's a bad investment."

He stared at her for a long moment. "That's a minimal way of putting it," he said finally. "Not that it matters, I suppose, whether it's a con or simply a bad investment— all the money will be gone anyway. But as it happens, I've met the oily snake who's selling it this time around, and I'm convinced it's a lot more than just a bad investment."

"So what do you expect me to do about it?" Deborah asked coolly. "And as far as that goes, why do you care? It isn't going to matter a snap to you if Ida throws away the family fortune."

"No. But I hate to see people taken for rides—especially when they didn't buy the tickets themselves. If Ida wants to fling away her own cash, that's one thing, every human being has the right to be a damn fool. But as trustee of the Lassiter Brothers money, she ought to be a little more careful."

"I'm charmed by your concern. Still..."

Riley sighed. "All right, I'll admit it, I do have a stake in it. The existing border of the Paradise Valley complex is just across the road from Mom's farm."

"I thought it was," Deborah murmured.

"And the oily snake is trying to buy the place from her."

"With Ida's cash? I don't see—"

"With no cash. He wants to give her stock in the corporation instead. Pretty little gold-edged certificates full of fancy writing."

"She can't just say no?"

"Of course she can. But she's not the only one whose land he's trying to buy, and other people, I'm afraid, aren't quite as farsighted as my mother is."

"Why so much land? I always thought Paradise Valley was a huge development."

"It is. But he wants to make it even bigger—private airstrip and parachute range and ski slopes."

"I thought you were kidding about the ski slopes. There aren't any hills on your farm."

"He's going to build some. At least he says he is."

"He's a big thinker."

"That, I believe, is what convinced Ida. It's all such a grand idea, and it would be delightful for Summerset if it actually ever got off the ground. It's hard not to be a believer when it all sounds so painless for the locals. After all—" there was an ironic twist to his voice "—he's got most of the money already, or at least he says he does, from big nameless investors on the East Coast. He's just offering the people of Summerset a chance to invest in themselves."

Deborah finished off her third muffin and absently reached for the last strip of bacon on Riley's plate. "I imagine you're looked on as something of a renegade, if you've been voicing these opinions."

He looked heavenward. "You might say. I'm a bit handicapped about speaking my mind, too."

"Why? Is business falling off at your restaurant?"

"I haven't noticed it. But the resort plans call for a rather large restaurant complex to be built in order to feed all those people, so..."

"So all of the resort's supporters think you're just screaming because you don't want the competition?" Deborah nodded wisely. "Now I see. No wonder you want me to tackle it. They aren't as likely to ride me out of town on a rail."

"Something like that." He reached across the table and let his long brown fingers brush the back of her hand. "If you'd just talk to Ida and get this thing stopped."

Deborah shook her head. "I don't see how that would do much good. Oh, it might save the Lassiter trust fund, but if he's already got money committed for the project..."

"Personally, I think the big investors are remaining nameless because they don't really exist. I think he's planning to gather up all the cash he can around Summerset and then disappear."

"Why buy all the land, then?"

"To increase his borrowing power, of course, by making his investors think he's rock solid. It certainly isn't costing him anything, and a list of those investors certainly looks appealing to others who might be wavering about handing over their life savings. The truth is, if Ida withdrew her support, the whole thing would collapse like the house of cards it is."

Deborah chewed thoughtfully at her lower lip. "Well, it's worth a try, I suppose."

"Good. Come down to Summerset and stay a couple of weeks, and see for yourself what's really going on. You can talk to her, you can meet the snake. As a matter of fact, it would be difficult for you to avoid meeting the snake, since he's moved into Ida's house."

"Riley, be realistic. I haven't seen Ida in three years, and even then it took her brother's funeral to get me there. I can't just come wheeling down there now out of the blue.

She's not a fool, she'll know why I'm there, and all the barricades will go up. I'll never get a word out of her.''

He shrugged. "It's simple. You're searching for artists."

"Is there an art exhibit in the town square this weekend?"

"Not that I've heard of, but—"

"Then be serious. For the first time in my years in business, I'm coming to Summerset on a whim to search for artists, and I just happen to choose the week after you've been in Chicago?" She nodded approvingly at his stricken look. "I see you've finally remembered that everyone in the whole town must know where you are."

"That is a problem," he conceded.

"I suppose I could pop up at the front door and scream, *Surprise!* but I think a better story would be useful." She caught a glimpse of his wristwatch. "Good heavens, I've got to get to work. I've got important things to do this morning. Let's finish this over dinner tonight."

"I thought you had a date."

"I do, with my father. Maybe he can help us figure it out."

"I don't think that's such a good—"

But she was gone, with a casual wave and a swirl of her tomato red skirt.

Riley sighed and reached for the bill and his wallet. "Important things," the waiter heard him say under his breath. "And this isn't?"

"I STILL DON'T THINK this is such a terrific idea," Riley said from the living room of Deborah's high-rise apartment, where he was coping with the cork in a bottle of white wine.

"I can't hear you," she called from the kitchen. "And I can't leave my béarnaise sauce just now."

He didn't answer, but he raised his voice. "Ida and your father never got along. She didn't think he was good enough for Vivien, you know."

"Is that what was going on? I wondered why he never seemed to be free when it was time for me to visit Aunt Ida."

"She also thought he was a hanger-on and a fortune hunter."

"Daddy? Surely you're joking."

"She would not be likely to take his advice on the subject of money."

The sauce was momentarily forgotten. Deborah leaned around the door to look at him in astonishment. "And you honestly think she'll take mine?"

"Not exactly. But she might be more careful about making sure there is some money left to leave to you. If it was only William, she'd probably spend it just for spite. The problem is, if you bring your father into it he may not be able to resist the temptation to call her up and scold her, or tell her what to do."

Deborah licked her tasting spoon thoughtfully. "And that would make her do the opposite?"

"I believe so, yes."

"Well, I think you're underestimating Daddy. He's developed into quite a diplomat since he went to work for the foundation." She waved a hand at the front door; the chimes were sounding. "In any case, he's arrived, so it's a bit late to dis-invite him, isn't it? My fingers are sticky...would you let him in?"

She retreated to the kitchen, catching her béarnaise sauce just as it started to curdle. A couple of minutes later

William joined her, a glass of sherry in his hand. "You're cooking, Deborah?"

"Well, I did promise you dinner. Would you be happier if I told you most of it came from the deli?"

"That's a relief. I thought you were trying to impress Riley. What's he doing here, anyway?"

She looked thoughtful. "Is that a trick question, like 'what did the bishop say to the actress?'"

"No, in fact, I'm delighted to see him. It's just that I seem to remember you saying when you were about fifteen that you'd never be caught dead in the same town with him again."

She stared into the distance, frowning. Then her brow cleared and she said, just as Riley came into the kitchen, "Oh, I remember. That was the summer I was in love with the lifeguard."

Riley handed her a glass of sherry. "You should see him now. You'd thank me for breaking it up."

"Don't take too much credit," Deborah ordered. "All you meant to do was embarrass me."

Riley grinned. "Well, you have to admit I succeeded in breaking it up. Whether I intended to or not isn't the point."

William shook his head. "This is not my idea of a usual family reunion," he said to no one in particular.

"And that's not the half of it," Deborah said. "Let me put the chicken on the grill and we'll sit down and talk about it."

William listened in almost utter silence throughout dinner. Deborah wondered about his unusual lack of comment, until she realized that the poor man couldn't get a word in over the dual explanation, and the accompanying bickering, to which he was being subjected. Finally, as she removed the men's gratifyingly empty plates and brought out a platter of fruit and cheese, William said simply, "I'm worried."

"Then she honestly can do it?" Deborah asked. "There aren't any safeguards?"

"Not anymore. Since Ralph died, Ida's been the boss."

"I told you," Riley said under his breath. "But you never would take my word for anything, Deb."

"And why on earth should I?" Deborah muttered. "You're the one who told me that if a woman swallows a whole shrimp it grows into a baby."

"You asked," he reminded. "I certainly wasn't the one who brought up the subject of where babies come from."

"I still don't like shrimp. Childhood prejudices can be very deep-seated, you know."

Riley appealed to her father. "She was six years old. What was I supposed to tell her? The truth?"

William went on, unheeding. "But Ida has always taken advice before, from her attorney and from her banker."

Riley shrugged. "And now she's taking advice from her investment counselor," he said. "She doesn't see that there's a difference, and she won't until it's too late and the Lassiter money has gone to Costa Rica, or wherever the crooks are hiding out these days."

Deborah stared into her wineglass, only half-listening. It was the first time she had really allowed herself to think about the consequences if Riley was right. The income supplied by the Lassiter trust wasn't as large as he supposed, but it was steady. And while the gallery was doing very well for a relatively new business, the overhead expenses of a location of Michigan Avenue were high, and every cent of profit went back into increased inventory. If she had to start paying her own living expenses from what the gallery brought in, she'd be in trouble all the way around.

"I may have to rely on those paintings you've been collecting to support my life-style after all, Daddy," she said morosely.

William didn't seem to be listening. "I wish I could remember the details," he mused. "I've got a copy of the entire trust document somewhere, but I'll be honest, I've always let the attorneys deal with the fine print rather than tangle with Ida. The income was always adequate, and so we didn't try to invoke the provisions for taking principal out."

"You can do that?" Riley sounded astonished. "That's the answer, then. You just get Ida to hand it over in lump chunks before she has a chance to throw it away."

William sighed. "It's not that easy, I'm afraid. The conditions for getting cash are strenuous. Old Jacob was determined to preserve what he'd gathered. I remember one, though." He smiled a little. "Vivien got a considerable sum when we were married."

"A marriage settlement?" Riley asked. "That makes sense. I always did think dowries were a civilized custom."

"That's not exactly what it was. It was to pay for the wedding, and for that purpose alone. And she even had to produce the bills to get the cash, at that. It seems old Jacob wanted the girls in the family to have wonderful weddings."

"Well, in his day marriage was the only profession women were allowed," Deborah pointed out.

"I don't think he even called it marriage, actually. The trust says something about dynastic alliances, I believe."

"Can we move on?" Deborah asked glumly. "This avenue is certainly getting us nowhere."

"Oh?" Riley asked. "You're not planning a large and elaborate wedding anytime soon? Though I don't suppose your friend with the fleecy face would go for—"

"Fleecy face?" William asked.

"He means Morgan," Deborah explained. "He's behind the times, but that never bothered Riley. More wine, anyone?"

Riley held up his glass. "I suppose you could talk to Ida's banker and her attorney," he said halfheartedly. "I didn't feel I could barge into their offices and start asking nosy questions, myself."

"It would be a source of information, perhaps," William said. "But I'm sure they're powerless to do anything."

"And probably just as frustrated as we are," Deborah mused. "And may I remind you that I still don't have a valid excuse for showing up in Summerset and starting to ask questions. I wonder...Ida's memory wouldn't happen to be slipping, would it?"

Riley snorted. "We should all be so alert at eighty. She plays bridge twice a week, she walks a mile every day, and she still chairs the hospital fund-raising drive."

"It was worth a try," she said.

"I'll look up that copy of the trust when I get home tonight," William said. "After all, Ida can't live forever. Surely Jacob considered the possibility."

Riley sounded a little disgusted. "If we don't concentrate on the problem at hand, it won't matter a damn whether Ida lives forever. Of course, Summerset might never be the same, but..."

"It's too bad we're all such law-abiding citizens," Deborah murmured. "If we weren't, we could just arrange for a hit-and-run on one of her long walks."

"Thank you," Riley said politely.

She stared at him. "I haven't any idea what you're talking about now."

"I'm touched that you've elevated me to the status of law-abiding citizen. I'll keep the memory of your kindness on the mantel among my trophies. Unless you thought I was going to volunteer to be the driver?"

She ignored him and started to clear the table.

"Well, I certainly didn't mean to imply anything of the kind," William said. He sounded hurt. "I would never set out to injure anyone. I've had my disagreements with Ida, but I've always shown her the respect due my wife's aunt."

"I'm sure you have," Riley said soothingly.

"And she always respected me as well, for Vivien's sake, if nothing else."

Deborah started to put the cheese plate away in the refrigerator. So things really had been bad between her father and Aunt Ida, she mused. If Ida had only put up with him for Vivien's sake . . .

Something seemed to stir in the back corner of her brain. *For Vivien's sake . . .*

She set the platter down very deliberately on the counter and went back into the dining room. "I've got it," she said.

Both of them looked up at her expectantly.

"I'm going to Summerset," she said.

"That's never been in doubt."

"Riley, would you shut up and listen? I'm not going to see Ida exactly, or at least not primarily to see her. I'm going down to introduce my intended husband and to talk to her about getting the trust to pay for my wedding."

William frowned.

"It's perfect, don't you see? That will force her to answer my questions about the trust."

"Great idea," Riley said enthusiastically. "Debbie darling, you might make a conspirator yet!"

"Deborah," her father said warily, "I don't think you've thought this through. I don't think that you and Bristol—"

"Bristol is out of town," she reminded him.

"Bristol?" said Riley. "Who the hell is Bristol? Never mind. Can you trust him not to spill the beans?"

"I won't have to. Bristol has nothing to do with this."

"Then who—"

She turned an expectant stare on Riley.

"Oh, Deborah," William began, "my dear girl—"

Riley said slowly, "If you're thinking of whom I think you're thinking of..."

"That's insane," William said uncertainly. "You can't pretend to be engaged to Riley."

"Why can't I? Do you already have a fiancée, Riley?"

"No. But—"

"Then acquiring one won't make any difference, will it?"

"But I don't want a fiancée!"

"Believe me, you won't have one for long. This is a very temporary measure. It was your mention of dynastic alliances that brought it to mind, Daddy. Reuniting the branches of a fractured family, restoring the family fortune, to say nothing of preserving the name to be carried on in generations to come. Ida will love it."

William said weakly, "But, Deborah..."

"It's a great idea, Daddy. And why shouldn't Riley make himself useful? He's already in the whole thing up to his—" She almost said ears, but thought better of it. "Neck. It even explains why he came to Chicago!"

Riley said faintly, "To see my long-lost love, I suppose you mean?"

"Absolutely." Deborah thought he sounded as if his collar were strangling him. Well, that was just too bad; he'd get used to the idea soon enough. It was such a satisfyingly symmetrical plot, after all.

And besides, she added, with a tiny secret smile, it was a world-class practical joke on Riley himself. Big enough to pay him back for every petty trick he'd pulled on her in all the years gone by....

AT FIRST she thought it was only Chicago traffic that was holding his attention so firmly, but long after they'd left the city behind and headed south for the tedious drive down the length of Illinois, Riley remained quiet, his eyes on the road, his hands steady on the wheel of her car.

She laid back her head against the leather upholstery and eyed him from behind her dark glasses. "I must say I always expected my fiancé would be a bit more excited than this on the day after our engagement became official."

Riley grinned. "Oh, but I am, Debbie darling. I'm having a wonderful day. It's the first time I ever drove a Jaguar, you know."

All right, she told herself, *you got exactly what you asked for, Deborah Ainsley!*

"It's going to take a bit of acting," she pointed out. "I think you're right that we don't dare take anyone in Summerset into our confidence, but we'll have to be very careful or no one will believe it at all."

"That we could actually be in love? I'll say."

"Let's not get personal, Riley. For one thing, we're going to have to curb the desire to grind each other into the dirt all the time."

His forehead furrowed. "No. I think we'd better just keep on acting normally, and simply give each other a longing look now and then, you know the sort of thing I mean.''

''In the hope that everyone will believe we're only teasing to hide the depth of our true feelings from the world?''

''Don't sound sarcastic. That's exactly what they'll think. Besides, I don't think we *could* stop scrapping, and the strain, if we tried, would be a dead giveaway.''

She looked at him long and steadily, and said, ''You're probably right. Now that I stop and think about it, Riley, I don't see you doing well in the role of Romeo.''

''Heaven forbid! 'What light through yonder window breaks? It is the east, and Debbie is the sun—' Forget it. I couldn't pull it off because I'd be laughing too hard.''

She decided not to bother answering that one.

''But longing looks I can handle,'' he added earnestly. ''I'll just stare at you and think of a filet mignon with duchess potatoes.''

''Thanks,'' Deborah said dryly. ''And if I see you're getting into trouble I'll just whisper 'chocolate mousse' in your ear.''

''That would be very thoughtful. Shall we practice?''

''What? The longing looks? You're driving, Riley.''

''I could pull off the highway. That looks like a truck stop up ahead, and truck stops almost always have very nice homemade pies.''

''Don't tell me, I already know. It's just research. Haven't you ever outgrown the need to eat every three hours?''

''No,'' he said simply. ''That's probably why the restaurant opportunity looked so appealing. And speaking of appealing, that sauce last night was—'' He took one hand off the wheel and kissed his fingertips in the best imitation of a comic-book French chef she'd ever seen. ''What did you call it?''

"Béarnaise. And it was curdled, Riley."

"Oh? That must be why I didn't recognize it," he said airily. "We serve a lot of it."

"I'll bet. Does this restaurant of yours have a name?"

"Yes. But mostly the locals just call it Riley's Place."

"That sounds like Summerset," she said gloomily. "A week there and I'll be raving."

"A week? I thought you were planning to stay two."

"I can't take that long. Besides, Aunt Ida would smell a rat if I could suddenly leave the gallery for that long."

"Even to spend time with your one true love?"

He sounded injured; she ignored him. "And third, Bristol will be back in ten days, so that's my outside limit."

"Does he live with you?"

"Of course not! I just—"

"I know—you don't want to explain this to him. Perhaps you should tell me about Bristol."

"Why?"

"Well, there are things we'd be expected to know about each other."

"Come on, Riley, the man I date?"

"The man you *used* to date," he corrected. "Remember? You're engaged to me now."

She groaned. "I suppose I have to start living the part. His name is R. Bristol Wellington, and he's the attorney for—"

"R. Bristol *which?* That sounds as if it needs a number to be complete."

"It has one," she said reluctantly. "He's the fifth."

"Oh? I suppose his ancestors came over on the *Mayflower?*"

"No, he considers that crowd to be peasants. Did you know you and I are third cousins, by the way? Bristol figured it out for me. He's very big on family."

"Yes, I can see that. Thoughtful of him. Who else?"

"That's about all, lately."

"I see. No wonder you didn't want to tell him about this."

"It's not that I wouldn't," Deborah defended herself. "In fact, I did tell him I was going to Summerset to see my aunt because talking to you again had prompted a wave of family feeling, and—"

The angle of Riley's eyebrows made her want to hit him. "I'll bet he liked that touch," he murmured. "It was probably a good idea to limit the details. He sounds like the humorless type."

"I didn't say he was anything of the sort. He would understand perfectly, but I . . ." She decided it was hopeless to try to explain to him that Bristol was serious and solid and dependable as the Rock of Gibraltar, and that she liked him just the way he was.

"What really did happen with you and the artist to make you settle down in this comfortable nonrelationship with Bristol?"

She wanted to groan. "You're not going to quit, are you? Just because I'm not living with the man. All right, I'll tell you. Morgan liked to keep his options open. He was like a man at a buffet dinner who takes a spoonful of everything because he doesn't want to miss out on something good."

Riley frowned. "I think I see. You mean that you wanted to settle down and he didn't?"

"Not only didn't he want to settle down," Deborah said dryly, "he seemed to think that women were like different varieties of macaroni salad, and he wanted to try them all."

He nodded thoughtfully. "That explains Bristol the fifth. No wonder he's so appealing to you."

She counted to ten and decided it was not necessary to give him a chance to explain that. "How about you, Riley? Any women in your life?"

"Oh, hundreds," he said airily.

"That's certainly helpful. Are there any I should watch out for in particular?"

His forehead wrinkled thoughtfully. "There are one or two who might consider poisoning your food, but I don't think they'll actually do it."

"What a comfort. I suppose the whole town is littered with your ex-girlfriends."

"Absolutely. By the way, that's quite a gallery you've got. Do you plan to sell it, or just close it down?"

She stared at him as if he'd suddenly grown antennae. "Sell it? Close it? Are you mad? I've worked myself to a thread for three years getting that gallery into shape. Why on earth would I give it up now that it's finally beginning to turn a profit?"

"You'll have to do something with it when you marry me and move to Summerset," he prompted gently. "Don't be a dunce, Debbie darling. You ought to expect to be asked that sort of question, you know."

"Not by you," she said a little sullenly. "When did you see the gallery, anyway?"

"I stopped on my way back to the hotel last night and peeked in the window. Good thing it was closed, too, window shopping is the only kind I could afford." He whistled.

She shook her head. "That's not true. I only buy originals, that's true, but there's a wide price range."

"The decorating scheme didn't look like it."

"Creating the look of success isn't cheap, Riley."

"So are you going to get out of the rat race and sell it?"

She shook her head. "Maybe you're the one who's going to move."

"To Chicago? Not me. Besides, if this is going to be your basic dynastic marriage, I have to stand firm, as the head of the household."

"Oh, for heaven's sake, Riley!"

"Pretend, darling. Practice saying it. 'When I marry Riley, I'm going to sell my gallery.'"

"Over my dead body. It's unique!"

He blinked. "The gallery, or the dead body? Never mind. Just repeat after me. 'And I'm probably going to have a dozen children....'"

Her practical joke was losing its flavor; it certainly seemed that Riley had adjusted himself to all the possibilities far better than she had managed to. "That's not funny," she muttered.

"You're the one who brought up passing on the name," he reminded.

"I always knew you were a chauvinist. You probably would expect your wife to stay home and raise the children."

"Stay home, no. Raise children, yes, I hope so."

"That's contradictory," Deborah complained. "Not that I expected anything else from you, but..."

"Why is it contradictory? I intend to change diapers, warm bottles at three in the morning, take out splinters—all the joys of parenthood—along with my regular job. Why shouldn't my wife have the same opportunity for a well-rounded life?"

She looked at him suspiciously. "That doesn't sound—"

"And stop trying to change the subject, anyway. I'm sure Ida will be thrilled at the idea of our beautiful and charming children. What would they be to her, anyway?"

"Great-great-nieces and nephews," Deborah said almost automatically. "And they'd all be redheads, too, I have no doubt. My God, Riley, that's a nightmare!"

He didn't seem to hear. "On your side, yes, they'd be nieces and nephews. But what about mine? I'm some sort of cousin."

"Who counts that far?"

Riley snapped his fingers. "I know," he said cheerfully. "We can just call up R. Bristol the fifth. I'm sure he'd be happy to figure it out for us."

CHAPTER THREE

AFTER THAT Deborah maintained a stern silence for almost twenty miles, until it became obvious that Riley didn't mind the sound of his own voice in the least, and if she wasn't going to talk to him he'd be quite happy to entertain himself. So she gave up the silent treatment, and the rest of the drive went by so quickly that she was startled when the car swept into the small city of Summerset, on the banks of the Summer River, and climbed steadily through the wide, uncrowded streets toward the highest point in town.

Lassiter House was by far the grandest private residence in Summerset; it rode the crest of the highest hill, reigning over the surrounding countryside. Now, in the midst of summer, it was hard to see it from a distance because of the trees that were far more numerous than people in Summerset, but in winter the house became a landmark that could be seen for miles.

Ostensibly, Jacob Lassiter had built his house atop the hill in order to catch the breezes from any direction, in the days when air-conditioning to battle the Midwest's relentless summer heat was still just a science-fiction dream. In actual fact, Deborah had always thought, he had liked the idea of sitting atop his hill like a feudal monarch on his throne, looking down upon his subjects. It had very nearly been a feudal town in Jacob's day, when half the workers in Summerset were employed by Lassiter Brothers, and the other half worked for the firms that provided food and clothing and services to them.

"You got awfully quiet all of a sudden," Riley said. "Are you mad at me again, or is it only nerves?"

"Neither. I was just thinking," she said. "I wonder if Jacob was ever happy up there, looking down on everyone."

"I imagine he sat up there with his binoculars and chortled while he watched the little ants scurry around, making his fortune grow."

"Do you really think so? I think perhaps he missed his brother, and regretted their quarrel."

Riley said shortly, "He had years to patch it up, if he regretted it. But he didn't bother."

She looked at him curiously. Had Bristol been right then? Did Riley nurse a grudge, and think that he and his family had been cheated?

Then he said, "What a romantic you are, Debbie darling."

She relaxed. "Perhaps. But I still think he must have missed the days when they lived side by side in the twin houses and walked to the factory together every day."

Riley made a sort of grunt. "I'm betting he didn't miss a thing. Well, there it is, in all its glory."

Lassiter House was a cross between a Swiss mountain chalet and a midsize cathedral. Or perhaps the architect had merely been working from Jacob Lassiter's mental image of those things, which he had never seen firsthand. It occupied almost the entire peak of the hill, and its three full stories, under a steep slate roof, seemed to extend the hill into a man-made mountain. The house was solid and massive and bulky, with flying buttresses supporting the side walls and holding up the huge balcony that stretched the width of the front. A carved frieze of grape leaves and mature bunches of fruit nestled under the roofline and rimmed the balcony railing, while stone gargoyles, each one with a different face, decorated the innumerable corners of the house.

Deborah muttered, "I've always thought that the architect should have gotten an award for inventing an entirely new style. They could have called it Early Horrible."

"Thank heaven it didn't start a trend," Riley said.

As the Jaguar flashed through the tunnel of huge old oak trees that lined the avenue at the base of the hill, the alternating light and shadow were like a strobe against Deborah's retinas and made her head ache. Then the car turned away from the sun and began to growl up the long winding drive, and she relaxed a little.

Riley parked the Jaguar in the small space that had been precariously carved out of the hillside for guest parking and came around to open her door. "What did Ida say when you called her?" he asked. "She isn't expecting that I'll be hanging around for dinner, is she? I really need to get back to work."

"Oh, I'm sure that won't be any problem," Deborah said airily. She looked up at the wide steps—a hundred of them, at least—that led up to the imposing front door and sighed; the parking lot was little more than halfway up the hill. "I suppose it would have ruined the view if old Jacob had allowed his friends to park on the front lawn. But still..."

"He did it on purpose, you know," Riley muttered. "This way anyone who came to see him and complain about something was immediately at a disadvantage, exhausted and out of breath."

"I'd forgotten how steep it was," she said a little later, gasping, and stopped for a moment on one of the wide terraced landings. "I used to run up and down this slope as if it was nothing. It's terrible, the things that happen as one ages, isn't it?''

"I hadn't noticed."

Deborah thought resentfully that it was probably true; he wasn't even breathing hard. It was with a great sense of relief that she finally put her finger firmly on the ornate old doorbell button. The chimes seemed to echo inside.

Riley had turned his back to the door to survey the view of the city. "Now this is where the ski slope ought to go," he said. "It's a natural."

The door creaked a little as it opened, and Ida Lassiter's man of all work appeared in the opening, a spotless white apron over his dark trousers and pristine white shirt, and a perfectly knotted black necktie in place. Riley had told her once that Henry slept in his necktie; Deborah had half believed him for years.

"May I— Miss Deborah!" The leathery old face wrinkled even more. "And Mr. Lassiter. Welcome home, Miss Deborah!"

The door swung wide and Deborah stepped across the threshold into Lassiter House. The great hall was cool and dim, despite the heat of the afternoon sun outside. It took a moment for her eyes to adjust, but she didn't need to see the room to know that it had not changed at all; something about the smell of it told her that. It was the same old slightly musty aroma that she remembered from the first time she had been brought here to spend the summer, when she was almost four. In the far corner was the dull gleam of the same polished armor that had terrified her as a child, and along the floor was the same worn old runner on which she had played hopscotch in rainy weather. And, she thought, the same old man, wearing, probably, the same old tie. Perhaps he really did sleep in it.

"I'll tell Miss Lassiter you've arrived," Henry said. "Is she expecting you?"

"Yes," Riley said.

"Not exactly," Deborah murmured at the same moment.

The old man's beady eyes shifted from one of them to the other without comment, and then he shuffled off down the hall.

"Poor Henry," Deborah said. "I thought at first that he hadn't changed at all, but he walks like a crab these days."

"What the hell do you mean, not exactly?" Riley said. "You told me you called her."

"No, I didn't. Tell you that, I mean."

He glared at her. The silence stretched out for a long moment. "All right," he admitted. "What you said was, she wasn't planning on me staying to dinner."

She nodded.

"Because you didn't even call her. Dammit, Deb!"

"I thought it would be better to take her by surprise," Deborah said with a shrug, "and not give her too much of a chance to think about it before we got here."

"Take her by surprise? Debbie, you utter fool! How could you?" He stopped and sighed. "Well, at least you accomplished one thing. Ida will have no trouble believing that you've been hanging around with me, under my evil influence. You've lost all your manners."

"I am in love," Deborah said with dignity. "Remember? That excuses a lot of things. But you're probably right about Ida's reaction. You never had any manners to speak of."

"I resent that accusation. My mother taught me to always speak kindly to ladies."

Deborah gave a genteel little snort. "Oh? By telling them they're utter fools?"

"If you are unfamiliar with my technique," Riley pointed out, "you might want to consider the possibility that it's because you're not exactly a lady."

Deborah thought she heard a step coming along the upstairs hall, a heavy, deliberate step. Now that it was too late to call off this ridiculous farce, now that she was within a minute of having to face Aunt Ida and spin out this impossible story, she began to feel a sick sort of squeamishness in the pit of her stomach.

"Maybe you should just run along, Riley," she muttered, "and let me handle this end of it. If you can't act the part—"

"You have doubts?" It was a very soft, very gentle murmur.

To the end of her days, Deborah would never quite know how she ended up held so firmly in Riley's arms that she couldn't have broken free with a bazooka. And when she looked up with flame in her eyes, astounded at finding herself so trapped, and began to protest, he silenced her with his mouth on hers, kissing her slowly and deliberately and not at all as if it was the first time ever, taking advantage of her unwitting, paralyzed cooperation to probe her mouth, his tongue exploring with infinite patience.

The sound of a throat being cleared, forcefully and loudly, brought her back to the edge of reality. *Aunt Ida,* she found herself thinking a bit vaguely, *must be having an attack if she can't even say anything. Seeing this sort of thing going on in her own front hall will probably leave her permanently scarred.*

Riley, who had his back to the stairs and who hadn't seemed to hear anything at all, just kept on kissing her. Deborah almost bit him, except that some tiny sane corner of her brain reminded her that however shocked Aunt

Ida might already be, things could always be made worse. So she kept her eyes closed tightly and tried to pretend that she was somewhere else altogether.

The throat was cleared again, even more loudly this time.

Deborah opened one eye, tentatively. Over Riley's shoulder she could see Aunt Ida standing on the bottom step, seeming to loom over the great hall. Her angular body was as straight and spare as ever. Her hair was the same wiry iron gray that it had been for as long as Deborah could remember. And the pose, with her arms folded squarely across her chest—that was familiar too; Deborah remembered it well from various scoldings.

Finally Riley relinquished her mouth, very slowly, and turned his head a bit. "Ida," he said, almost as if he'd seen a ghost. "I'm so sorry. I got carried away, I'm afraid. You see, your niece has just promised to make me the happiest man in the world."

His words were ever so slightly slurred, as if passion had indeed gotten out of hand. It was a good performance, Deborah had to admit, as long as he didn't overdo it and end up sounding instead as if he'd had to too much to drink.

"She's planning to make you happy in private, I trust," said a familiar raspy voice, almost masculine in tone, "and not in my front hall. It would shock Henry."

Riley laughed sheepishly. "Didn't I make myself quite clear? I mean she's promised to marry me."

There was a half snort from the direction of the staircase. "These days, one never knows what a young woman might mean. So that's what brings you home to Summerset, young lady."

Deborah didn't answer. *Obviously,* she was thinking, *I overestimated the extent of Aunt Ida's shock. It doesn't seem to have bothered her at all. I wonder . . .*

Riley pinched her. Deborah jerked back to reality, decided that stomping on his toes would not be appropriate, however inviting the temptation, and smiled at Aunt Ida. "I just couldn't wait to let you know how happy I am," she said in the most oozingly sweet voice she could muster. She thought the sound of it made Riley look a little ill.

"Speak up," Ida commanded. "Don't mumble so, Deborah."

Deborah sighed and said a little louder, "Of course I'm anxious to get the wedding plans under way, and I couldn't possibly do that without your advice. I can only spare a week right now, but I'm sure—"

"Well, come here," Aunt Ida ordered. "Surely you can leave your young man for long enough to give me a dutiful kiss."

It was only then that Deborah realized she was still firmly within the circle of Riley's arms, so closely nestled against his body that she seemed to have been glued there. It took physical effort to move away from the illusion of safety that he represented and take the few steps that brought her to Ida's side. The hug they shared was brief, stiff and a little awkward; Ida had not come down off her step, and her sharp chin dug uncomfortably into Deborah's scalp. It was a relief when the social amenity was fulfilled and Deborah could stand on her own again.

"You've had lunch, of course," Ida announced. It was not a question. "In any case, I couldn't invite you. Henry has far too much to do without being a short-order cook."

Deborah wanted to wince; the remark was so obviously an arrow aimed at Riley. Perhaps, she thought, she'd been wrong after all about Ida's reaction to dynastic alliances;

the woman hadn't seemed thrilled with the news. But she restrained the retort she'd have liked to make and said mildly, "Yes, we've had lunch."

"Then we'll let Riley go on about his business—I'm sure there are things needing his attention—while we have a chat," Ida said. She started down the long dim hall. "As for dinner, I'll have to tell Henry right away. An extra guest does complicate things for him, you know."

Riley winked at Deborah behind Ida's back and called after the old woman, "You needn't worry about feeding Debbie. She's having dinner with me tonight at the restaurant."

Deborah made a face at him.

"In fact," he went on, "I thought perhaps we'd celebrate with an impromptu engagement party, Ida—you, my mother, the two of us. . . ."

Ida stopped but didn't turn around. "Yes, that would be very nice. But I'd hate to leave my guest alone, and it's just as hard on Henry to have to cook a meal for one as it is to have unexpected extras."

Riley smiled wryly at Deborah, who was wide-eyed with astonishment. "Bring him along," he said, and added under his breath, "After all, he's almost part of the family. Now do you see what I mean, Debbie, my dear?"

IT WASN'T A CHAT so much as it was a machine gun firing of questions, with Ida not listening to—or perhaps not even hearing—the answers. The third time Deborah was ordered not to mumble, she found herself longing to ask Aunt Ida how long it had been since her hearing was checked, but she controlled the impulse and repeated the answer instead. She might as well not have bothered, however; by that time, Ida was off on another train of thought altogether.

"I assumed you'd marry some high-powered lawyer or stockbroker or something in Chicago," she said.

"Oh, I've dated a few people like that. But you see, Aunt Ida, there's just no one like Riley." *And that,* Deborah thought piously, *is certainly the truth!*

Ida did not seem sympathetic to the idea of young love. "I hope you both realize that the Lassiter trust isn't going to support you. The income you're already getting is all there will be."

I should be glad that she brought the subject up herself, Deborah thought, *even though the way she did it makes me want to chew nails.* "I assumed that," she said calmly. "But while we're talking about the trust, just what is the money intended for? I understand that there may be some funds to help pay for our wedding."

Ida's eyes narrowed. "William told you that, no doubt. I suppose that means he's used up his last dime and couldn't even afford to give you a ride to the church."

"Daddy's doing very well, thank you," Deborah said stiffly.

Ida snorted. "Well, I haven't time for an analysis of the situation just now. I have a bridge tournament this afternoon." She rose, straight and imposing. "We'll talk about it later."

Deborah retreated to the guest room at the head of the stairs with relief. It was going to take some time to readjust, that was all, she told herself. She simply wasn't used to Aunt Ida's abrasiveness.

As soon as she saw the vintage Rolls depart, with Ida sternly upright in the back seat and Henry hunched over the wheel, Deborah stopped unpacking, changed her cotton dress for brief shorts and a halter top and returned to the brick patio behind the house with a book and a glass of iced spring water, luxuriating in the knowledge that for the next three hours peace would reign over Lassiter House.

It actually lasted for a little less than three minutes.

The first indication of trouble was a bright red beach ball that sailed over the fence and landed with a soft splash at the edge of the swimming pool. Deborah looked up with a frown and studied the ball over the top of her sunglasses for a long moment, watching it bob gently in the water.

A couple of minutes later a head appeared over the brick wall that surrounded patio and pool. It was topped with a thatch of white-gold hair, and it was followed by a wiry body that scrambled over the top of the wall and landed with a small thud on the bricks. The boy was about seven or eight, she thought, and she watched quietly from her corner as he dusted off the seat of his shorts, kicked off his shoes and headed for the water.

Then she put down her book and tugged off her sunglasses. "Excuse me," she said.

He wheeled around to face her, with stark terror in his wide brown eyes; the freckles on his face stood out like tattooed dots.

"What on earth are you doing here?" Deborah asked. "This is private property."

The calmness of her question seemed, in an odd way, to reassure him. "I had to come and get my ball. It flew over the fence."

Deborah studied him for a long moment—the wiry body, the small, square face with a cleft in the chin. "Accidentally, I'm sure," she said. "While you were playing."

The boy nodded hopefully.

"But the question is, where were you playing? Unless you threw it all the way up here from the bottom of the hill, you must have been on Miss Lassiter's property."

He shuffled his bare feet on the bricks. "Well, how was I supposed to know you were here?" he asked reasonably. "You didn't even squeak when I threw the ball over the fence. If you had, I'd have been downtown before you ever saw me."

Deborah stifled her desire to giggle at this disarming honesty, but it took effort. "You've got quite a system figured out, haven't you? Have you lost a lot of beach balls that way?"

"Only a couple," he said modestly. "She goes off every Friday, and most Tuesdays, and sometimes on Thursdays, too."

Deborah shook her head. "I don't believe it," she said to no one in particular. "Under her very eyes..."

The boy gulped. "Are you going to turn me over to her? To the witch?"

She hid her smile. Ida Lassiter as the town witch... yes, she could see how that legend might have grown. "To be made into mincemeat pie or something? She's not that bad, you know, she's just not used to kids. She never was." It was true, she thought, with a hint of surprise; much of Ida's sternness, which had so terrified her as a child, could well have been uncertainty, instead, or a fear of embarrassing herself. *Don't break your heart over it,* she told herself abruptly. *She's still acting the same way!*

The French doors from the sun room opened, and a male voice said, "Ida? Have you someone here with you?" Then the man in the doorway saw Deborah on the chaise longue, and the voice warmed as he came quickly across the patio. "Well, you must be Deborah. Aren't you? I recognized you from the portrait in Ida's sitting room. I'm Preston Powell. I had no idea you were here. I am so pleased to meet you."

Preston Powell, she thought. The man Riley referred to as the oily snake.

He didn't look like a con man, she had to grant him that. He was older than she had expected, in his early forties, perhaps, with a distinguished touch of premature silver at his temples. His big blue eyes were wide and ingenuous and, at the moment, very admiring. His golf clothes were brightly colored, but neat and well pressed—by Henry, she had no doubt. And he didn't look the slightest bit oily, or serpentine.

But then, Deborah told herself, no real con man looked like the movie stereotype, or he couldn't possibly make a living. The fact that the man looked like an older version of a Botticelli angel certainly didn't make him innocent.

His eyes fell on the child. "You again," he said. "You've been hanging around and annoying people long enough, and now I find you here. I ought to have charges filed against you."

The child's wide eyes turned to Deborah with a wordless appeal. He was actually terrified, she realized. "There's no need for that," she said mildly. "The young man is merely keeping me company this afternoon."

Preston Powell's eyes warmed again. "If I'd known you were here, and realized it was company you wanted..."

She put her glasses back in place on her nose and picked up her book. "I'm sure you're too busy developing Paradise Valley to spend the afternoon with me." Then she wanted to bite her tongue, because her words seemed to intrigue him.

"Has Ida told you about our plans, then?"

Deborah's heart sank. Riley was right; Ida *was* in it up to her Roman nose.

"I'd be happy to tell you all about it," he went on confidentially, "but right now I have a very important golf date. The whole future of the development may depend on it. If it wasn't so important, rest assured that I'd break my appointment just because you asked me to. . . ."

She refrained, with an effort, from pointing out that she hadn't asked him to do anything of the kind, and reminded herself that she needed all the information she could get about Mr. Preston Powell, and if being polite to him was the best way to get it, then she'd just have to bite her tongue and be polite. "Some other time, then," she said. "I'll look forward to it."

She wouldn't have been surprised if he had kissed her hand before he finally got himself back into the house.

"Gee," the child began in a disgusted voice, "I don't think—"

Deborah silenced him with a finger across her lips, and pointed to the water in a wordless command. He frowned, but he plunged in, and a few minutes later, over the sound of splashing, she heard a car leave the garage and growl down the hill.

The child heard it, too, and he pulled himself up to the side of the pool. "He's gone," he announced.

"And not a bit too soon. What's your name?"

"Alec Chastain."

"And what did Mr. Powell mean about you hanging around?"

The child shrugged. "I offered to wash his car for a couple of dollars. But I wasn't on the property, honestly, I wasn't. I was down at the bottom of the hill. I don't know why he got mad about that."

Deborah could guess; that had sounded like a very high-performance engine. She wouldn't care to turn over her Jaguar to this infant for tender loving care, that was certain. And yet . . .

Alec climbed out of the water. "Thank you for not giving me away," he said politely. "My mom would kill me if I got in trouble. No, she wouldn't, exactly. She'd just look at me that way she has. . . ." His voice trailed off. "Would you mind if I went out the gate? It's a little tricky climbing the wall when I'm wet."

Deborah didn't look at him. She turned a page and said casually, "If your mother objects, why do you do it?"

From the corner of her eye she could see him shrug his thin shoulders. "The town pool has a crack in it, and all the water leaks out as soon as they put it in, so it's been closed all year. And we can't afford to belong to the country club. So there's no place to swim, and I miss it a lot."

"And meanwhile this pool just sits here unused." She wondered why Ida had bothered to fill it this year. In this climate an open pool, surrounded by trees, was more nuisance than pleasure, and Ida was not a swimmer.

Alec nodded. "He uses it a lot." From the tone of his voice there was no doubt whom he meant. "It's a nice pool." With his bare toe, he traced the pattern of one of the ceramic tiles that lined the edge.

"It used to have pillars all around it, in a bad imitation of a Roman bath. I've been told it was the first swimming pool in town, and when it was built it had saltwater in it."

Alec wrinkled his nose. "That sounds awful."

"Thus speaks a Midwestern child. It's just like swimming in the ocean."

"Is it? I've never seen an ocean." His voice was wistful.

Deborah looked quickly down at her book. *Lots of kids haven't been to the ocean,* she told herself. *Don't get all sentimental about it!*

"Thank you for letting me swim," Alec said. He retrieved his beach ball.

"I told Mr. Powell you were spending the afternoon with me," Deborah said, without looking up. "So don't make a liar out of me. Back in the water, kid."

"I can? Honest?"

He'd have hugged her if she hadn't fended off his wet embrace. "I'm not promising anything in the future," she warned. "But for this afternoon, at least."

He spent most of the time in the water, but in the intervals he stretched out on the tiles beside her chair, and talked with the easy confidence of a longtime friend. Deborah heard all about school, and how glad he was that it was summer, and why he and his mother had come to Summerset after Alec's father died two years ago. In his voice Deborah could hear how tough the loss and the move had been on both of them. But he didn't seem to want sympathy; he stated the facts, and then skipped on to talk of Paradise Valley and how wonderful it would be when the resort was finished. Perhaps he could caddy at the golf course then, he said, and learn to water-ski on Paradise Lake.

Poor Alec, she thought. Despite his experience with Preston Powell, he seemed to see no contradiction between the promising plans and the anything but generous man who stood behind them. She wondered how many others in Summerset felt the same as Alec did. No wonder Riley was so concerned.

And when, she wondered, was she going to get a chance to talk to Riley again? Not at dinner, that was certain, with his mother and Ida and Preston Powell there, too.

Dinner, she thought with a sigh, and wondered if she should go raid Henry's refrigerator for a snack. Lunch had been bad enough; watching Riley eat a cheeseburger at a roadside truck stop where the closest thing to healthy food had been a fish of uncertain ancestry, pressed into a patty and deep-fried. She hated to even think about dinner.

Well, it was only a week, after all, and she'd be back in Chicago with Bristol, and she could have quail at Coq au Vin.

She could almost taste it.

PRESTON POWELL'S CAR turned out to be a Cadillac, pure white with a dark red leather interior. Deborah had to admit she wouldn't have turned it over to Alec for washing, either, but it didn't make her feel any more charitable toward Preston. And when he carefully ushered Ida into the front seat, but told Deborah with an expressive look that he wished it could have been her beside him instead, she wanted to bite something, or someone. Ida, perhaps, because she obviously had not told him of Deborah's supposed engagement.

Instead, she smiled sweetly and then settled back and pretended to watch with fascination as Summerset sped by. Still, she could see from the corner of her eye that he was spending more time looking at her in the driving mirror than he was watching the road. It wasn't her imagination, either; even Aunt Ida had a tart comment about it, and for a couple of minutes Preston seemed to concentrate very carefully on the traffic. But soon he was addressing Deborah again.

She began to wonder how far they could possibly be going, and she wished that she'd had the sense to ask Riley a few more questions about that blasted restaurant of his. He *had* said it was in Summerset, hadn't he?

No, she realized belatedly. He hadn't. Not exactly, at least.

The Cadillac slowed on the main avenue and turned down one of the city's original, narrow, brick-paved streets running toward the Summer River. Deborah frowned. There was nothing much down here except warehouses, which had been abandoned long ago when the riverboat trade dropped off.

But at least one of them was abandoned no longer; that was obvious from the number of cars that surrounded the tall, narrow old building. A discreet sign proclaimed that the place was now offering food and drink, and as the Cadillac drew up before the front door with a flourish, a young man in a dark green uniform sprang from the doorway and opened the passenger doors. He assisted Ida from the car, while Preston came around to help Deborah out. She stood on the sidewalk for a moment and stared at the building. This was what the natives called Riley's Place?

"Your car," she said automatically as Preston offered his other arm to Ida and started toward the door. But behind her the Cadillac's engine revved gently as the young man moved it away from the entrance.

Valet service, she thought helplessly. In a town like Summerset?

Inside the building it was invitingly dim, lit with the softness of candle glow. On the moss green walls of the foyer were old advertising signs, interspersed with a series of antique botanical prints that almost took Deborah's breath away.

A young blond woman in a severe dark blue cocktail dress greeted them with a professional smile, which flickered as she recognized Ida and faltered altogether for an instant when she saw Deborah.

Ah, Deborah thought. *This must be one of the young women who wouldn't mind poisoning my food. He's obviously broken the news to this one, at least.*

The young woman led them past a cocktail lounge full of mirrors and crystal and stained glass, and through a dining room with tables draped in peach and moss green linen, to a smaller room at the far side of the building, with wide windows overlooking the river. A small group was already there: Riley's mother and a man with a shock of iron gray hair who Deborah decided must be her new husband. And, turning to greet them, Riley, in dinner clothes. The stern black and white, lightened with a moss green tie and cummerbund, made his hair look like burnished copper. He looked wonderful, Deborah thought. And also... comfortable, that was the word. As if he practically lived in dinner clothes.

She looked around the room. More botanical prints, more incredible antiques. Against one wall was a small table of hors d'oeuvres, their delicate fragrances filling the air. Nearby was a silver wine bucket, with a bottle already chilling.

This, she thought, was far from being the half café, half bar that she had expected. It wasn't even simply a restaurant. And Riley had given her no warning.

It's inevitable, Deborah thought. *Sooner or later, I'm going to kill him. And at the rate he's going, it isn't likely to be later.*

CHAPTER FOUR

RILEY'S SMILE of greeting was slightly tinged with mischief, she thought, but then that was nothing new. And there was certainly nothing to criticize about the way he kissed her cheek—lightly, but just lingeringly enough to suggest that he wished he didn't have such a large audience—before he greeted Ida and Preston Powell.

Deborah crossed the room to Riley's mother with a combination of relief and genuine pleasure. During the long summers with Aunt Ida, Anna Maria Lassiter had sometimes been Deborah's salvation, and the big old white farmhouse had been a welcome change from the stiffness of Lassiter House—except, of course, for Riley's presence. Out on the farm, it had been possible to dig a hole halfway to China without repercussions, or to make a horrendous mess in the kitchen under the guise of hosting a tea party—things that, according to Ida, proper little girls didn't do. At least, not in her garden, or her kitchen.

So it was with genuine gladness that Deborah hugged Anna Maria, noted with a hint of sadness the lacy map of lines in the woman's face and was introduced to her new husband.

"Well, not *new,* exactly," Alan Holmes told her with a twinkle in his dark eyes. "Rather shopworn, I'm afraid, and my guarantee ran out long ago. I warned Anna Maria of that before she married me, but you know how women are. Once they make up their minds what they want, logic doesn't enter into it anymore."

Deborah laughed and fluttered a hand toward Riley, in the far corner of the room. "I know," she murmured. "The same sort of thing has happened to me."

"Oh, it's not the same at all," Anna Maria said solemnly. "Riley comes with my personal guarantee—I promise that whatever happens, he'll do the unexpected."

"And in this case, I'm the unexpected," Deborah murmured.

Anna Maria smiled. "Yes, you are, though I didn't mean it to sound that way. The sparks you two used to strike off each other...who would have thought it would end up like this? But Deborah, I'm so glad!"

And she genuinely was, too, Deborah thought uneasily. No one could fake such sincerity, certainly not the forthright Anna Maria. There was going to be disappointment down the road....

Never mind, she told herself. *If we manage to keep Preston Powell from putting the whole town in his pocket and walking off with it, any disappointment Anna Maria feels in the end will certainly be tempered with understanding.*

A waitress in a dark green dress was scurrying around, bringing their before-dinner drinks. Deborah had asked for her favorite brand of sparkling water, a rather obscure imported variety, and she was not surprised when it appeared. Nothing much about this place would surprise her now, she thought.

She glanced at the table, set for six. "Isn't Mary Beth coming?" she asked.

Anna Maria shook her head. "She and Rod are giving a dinner party tonight. He's a partner now in his law firm.

She hated having to miss it, though. If Riley had only let her know—''

''It was my last-minute idea to come with him,'' Deborah interrupted. ''I told him it was so he didn't have to cope with the commuter train, but the truth is, when it came right down to saying goodbye...'' She tried to look girlishly shy.

Anna Maria smiled fondly.

And that's another one you owe me, Riley Lassiter, Deborah thought.

''Mary Beth is very eager to see you. I think she's dying to hear all about your wedding plans. Perhaps we can all get together at the farm tomorrow.'' She sounded almost diffident. ''We've made a lot of changes out there, and I'd like you to see them. Of course if you don't have time...''

''Not have time to see the farm? I couldn't live with myself if I missed that.'' She listened for a moment to Ida's brusque, too loud voice. From all the way across the room she could hear something about resort financing. She sighed. ''As long as I don't have to bring Aunt Ida and her sidekick with me.''

Anna Maria smiled wryly. ''You've heard, then, about the uproar? It's splitting the town, I'm afraid. Half the population are convinced they'll make their fortunes with Paradise Valley stock. The other half, well, no matter how it turns out it won't be pretty.''

''Anna Maria, your prejudice is showing,'' her husband warned.

''I know, and this is not the place to discuss it.''

''Certainly not with the sidekick coming this way,'' Deborah murmured.

''And why Riley included *him* in your engagement dinner is beyond me.''

"You know Riley, always doing the unexpected." Deborah sipped her sparkling water.

Anna Maria broke into the brilliant smile that lit up her eyes and erased the lines from her face.

"Mrs. Holmes," Preston Powell exclaimed. He would have kissed her, Deborah thought, but Anna Maria's Manhattan glass was suddenly and inexplicably in the way, just where it could tip and dump its contents down the front of his bold plaid jacket if he wasn't careful. He settled for seizing her free hand and shaking it with gusto. "I've tried to get back to you in the past few days, but it's been so busy that I haven't had a chance."

"I hadn't given it a thought. I'm a bit busy myself these days, Mr. Powell."

"Oh, call me Preston, please. I've been thinking about our last talk, and I believe that perhaps I could do a little better on my offer for your land. After all, there is no sense in my pretending—it's a key piece of property." He put a hand on her arm and went on earnestly, "And of course, while we could do without it, it would make things much more difficult if we had to build the resort around you."

Anna Maria smiled. It was not her heart-stopping, genuine smile, but something cool and remote. "Good," she said sweetly.

For a split second Preston Powell looked confused. Then he laughed. "For a moment there, I thought you meant... We'll get together this week about my new offer."

Deborah wondered for a moment if the man was honestly so dense. *No,* she thought. *He can't be. He knows quite well what Anna Maria means, he's just not going to go down without a fight.*

"Shall we sit down?" Anna Maria led the way to the table and took her seat at the end of it.

Deborah found her hand caught in Riley's; he seated her next to him, with a flourish. "What do you think, Debbie darling?" he murmured in her ear.

He couldn't have heard his mother's exchange with Preston Powell; he'd been too absorbed with Ida. So Deborah didn't pretend to misunderstand. "You know perfectly well what I think of your little restaurant." But she managed to smile sweetly as she said it, in case anyone was watching her. "You could have warned me, Lassiter."

"Admit it, Deb," he said as he pulled out his own chair. "You had this picture of me as a short-order cook in a greasy apron slopping out hash browns and eggs sunny-side up, didn't you?"

She looked meaningfully across the table at Aunt Ida, who was absorbed in her menu.

Riley didn't seem to notice. "It was too delicious an opportunity. I simply couldn't resist it. Anyway, you should take it as a compliment."

"A compliment?"

"Yes." It was a bare murmur. "I have so much trust in you now, after this afternoon, that I had no doubt that you could carry off a surprise with class. And I was right."

There was no answer to that, at least none that was safe considering the company they were keeping. So she smiled lovingly at him and jabbed his ankle with her spike heel instead.

He turned his gasp of pain into a cough.

"One surprise deserves another," she said pleasantly.

Aunt Ida looked up thoughtfully from the menu. "Do you have lobster tonight, Riley?"

"Certainly. They were flown in just this afternoon."

Ida leaned back in her chair expansively. "That's what I'm having, then. It's my favorite." She beckoned to the waitress. "Bring out a couple so I can choose. I like the liveliest ones, so don't bother to bring any that just lie there. Deborah, you've never tasted anything so wonderful as Riley's lobster."

Deborah shuddered a little. "I'll pass. I know it's silly, but I can't bear eating something that has actually looked at me."

"First it was shrimp," Riley murmured, "and now you're turning down lobster as well? And you wouldn't have a cheeseburger for lunch, either. My dear girl, you're missing out on the best things in life."

"What was that?" Aunt Ida asked. "Don't mumble, Riley. It's very rude."

Next to Ida, Alan Holmes raised his glass. "A toast to the new couple," he said. "To Deborah and Riley—may your life together be filled with happiness!"

Beside Deborah, Preston Powell frowned, but he raised his glass. "A new couple?" he said, over the clink of crystal. "That's hardly sporting, Deborah. You're not even wearing a ring."

Riley's eyebrows went up, but he merely said, "Thanks for reminding me, Powell. Debbie, bless her heart, hasn't even said a word about it."

Deborah thought, *That's largely because Debbie-bless-her-heart forgot all about little things like engagement rings, and the fact that everyone will expect her to have one. Damn, I should have picked up something from my jewel box. Anything would have done. These days nearly any crazy thing can be an engagement ring.*

Riley dug into his pocket. "And even though this doesn't have much monetary value, darling, I know you'll treasure it the same way I do—for the sentimental attachment it carries."

On his palm lay a dark maroon box, so worn along the edges that the nap was gone from the velvet covering. Deborah looked at it with something that was almost dread.

Then she reached for the box and told herself firmly, *No, he wouldn't have booby-trapped it.*

But she held it for a moment anyway, assuring herself that it was safe to open. No tiny fake rattlesnake would leap out at her. No water would spray in her face. No horrible noise would greet the opening of this box. There was too much at stake here for Riley to indulge himself in a childish practical joke. Besides, he'd outgrown all that nonsense, hadn't he?

She held her breath and pressed the catch.

Inside the velvet box, on a bed of gold satin creased and cracked with age, lay a narrow gold band that held a single small diamond, hardly more than a chip. It was obviously antique; the style was that of a generation long gone. But the ring itself looked almost new. The gold was bright and unscratched, and the etched lines that formed the only decoration in the metal were deep and unworn.

Riley picked up her hand and slipped the ring onto her finger. It almost fit, and it was so light that she hardly knew it was there. He looked into her eyes as if he'd like to drown himself in them.

With an unholy desire to giggle, she told herself, *Remember, he's thinking of filet mignon.*

"Thank you for waiting," he said, loud enough that even Aunt Ida could hear. He held her hand to his lips, and Deborah thought she saw his mother wipe away a clandestine tear.

Aunt Ida cleared her throat. "How very touching. I suppose this is going to be the splashiest wedding Chicago ever saw."

Deborah nodded.

At precisely the same instant, Riley shook his head.

She turned to glare at him, and he caught himself up short. "Not Chicago," he said smoothly. "We'll be married here in Summerset."

Deborah sighed inwardly. She supposed it was the best recovery he could have made, but still—

"Well, that will make it easier," Ida rasped. "All you have to do then is beat Mary Beth's record."

"We're not interested in competing, Aunt Ida," Deborah said in soothing tones. "Still, one's wedding day only comes once, and it's the most important day in a woman's life. It should be perfect. I've got my heart set on a big wedding—I must have ten friends who'll want to be bridesmaids."

Not at any wedding I'm participating in, Riley seemed to be thinking. At least, to Deborah's eyes, he looked a little sour.

She plunged on recklessly. "And a big reception, of course, and a dance..."

"Here at Riley's place." Ida gave a rusty laugh. "You've shown good sense there, girl. At least you won't need a caterer. Though you'd better be careful with the menu. If it gets too complicated, it might keep him from getting to the church at all, and you certainly wouldn't want that!"

ANNA MARIA AND ALAN were the first to go, pleading an early start to their days now that the vegetable harvest was in full swing. Ida and Preston followed. They seemed a little reluctant to leave Deborah behind, but Riley assured them that he would bring her home soon.

"With what?" Deborah asked suspiciously as soon as the older couples were gone. "I wouldn't put it past you to have a saddle horse tucked away somewhere. Or a donkey cart.''

Riley laughed. ''Nothing so mundane, I'm afraid. Just your Jaguar. Hadn't you noticed it wasn't up at Lassiter House?''

''You stole my car? Why, you—''

''Of course not. Surely you didn't expect me to walk all the way down here with my luggage. Just let me check on how things are going in the restaurant and we can slip off for a quiet chat. I think we need one, don't you? All this craziness about a wedding. It sounds more as if you're planning an average-size coronation!''

He was gone before she could protest. She sat down at the table again, tapping her fingers impatiently against the cloth.

The waitress returned with a cart and said, ''Oh, I'm sorry. I thought everyone was gone.''

''Don't let me hold up your work.''

''If you're certain you don't mind...''

Deborah saw fine lines of fatigue around the woman's eyes. Quickly and competently she began to clear the dessert dishes, and without a word Deborah followed suit.

The waitress gave her a startled look, but not until all the dishes were on the cart and she was replacing the tablecloth with a fresh one did she speak. ''Someone told me you run an art gallery in Chicago, Miss Ainsley.''

Deborah decided she might as well get the worst over with. Riley had warned her there would be such questions, after all. ''Yes,'' she said. ''But not for long.''

''Oh?''

''When Mr. Lassiter and I are married, I'll give it up, of course.'' *And a good thing it is,* she thought, *that Mr. Lassiter and I aren't ever going to make it to the altar!*

"Oh. Of course." The fresh tablecloth was precisely in place, and the waitress started to wheel the loaded cart toward the door. "I just wanted to tell you congratulations, Miss Ainsley. Riley is a wonderful man, you know."

Riley, Deborah thought. How democratic of him. Or, perhaps, was this another of the women who wouldn't mind poisoning Deborah's food? The waitress wasn't exactly a child, but she couldn't be past thirty, and she would be attractive if she didn't look so tired. Preston Powell had noticed, that was sure; he'd spent most of the evening flirting with her.

The waitress went on, "Riley is—"

"Back," he said gently from the doorway. "So please, no more applause. It will give me a big head. Thanks, Ruth, you did a wonderful job tonight."

The woman seemed to glow just a little. Deborah found it fascinating.

Riley led her to a wide stairway that stretched up into the dark recesses of the warehouse. At the second landing he stopped for a moment and tugged his tie loose, then unfastened the top button on his shirt with a sigh of relief.

"Where are we going?" she asked doubtfully.

He gave a villainous chuckle. "To my private lair."

"I can't wait, but do you suppose you could stop taking your clothes off till we actually get there? The contrasting styles of dress made dinner a bit uncomfortable, I'll admit, but you've gone quite far enough now to put me at ease—"

His fingertips touched the shoulder of her white cotton dress as if brushing a bit of lint away. "You were uncomfortable in this? It's a very pretty dress."

"But a bit casual, compared to your costume. I thought all the men in Summerset believed that formal dress meant wearing trousers and shoes instead of denim overalls and work boots.''

His eyes lit appreciatively. ''Most of us still do.''

He turned an elaborately carved brass doorknob and ushered her into a large room lit only by moonlight pouring through huge windows that looked out over the river.

''And if you were uncomfortable because I didn't warn you about the restaurant,'' he went on reasonably, ''you deserve it. You should have told me you hadn't bothered to call Ida.''

That was true enough, she reflected. ''Still, it could have been nasty if I hadn't kept my head.''

''A minor fight between us now and then will add realism to the whole situation. If you had blown up, I'd have abased myself at your feet, and we'd have patched it back together. Then a few weeks from now when we call the whole thing off, everyone would say, 'Yes, we saw this coming when they had that fight the night of their engagement dinner.' ''

Deborah frowned. ''And they wouldn't think to ask whether we'd been telling the truth all along?''

''Something like that.''

''Then you don't plan to tell them eventually that it was all a hoax?''

''Why should we? We'll have gained what we wanted, so why embarrass everybody who fell for the trick?''

''You'd actually rather have your friends think you were jilted than know the truth?''

In the moonlight and shadow, his smile gleamed. ''But Debbie darling, who says I'm the one who's going to be jilted?'' He snapped a couple of lamps into dim life, casting pools of soft light across the polished expanse of a wide oak plank floor. An overstuffed couch and two deep chairs were gathered in the center of the room, on a geometrically printed rug. The rest of the huge space was practically empty. Some of the walls were the old, random brick of the original structure; others had been covered with stucco left its natural neutral shade. They were all bare.

"Obviously the person who decorated the restaurant has never been up here," Deborah murmured.

"Of course she has." He poured two glasses of cognac and waved a hand at the couch. "She keeps making noises about wallpaper. Personally I think I should decide where to put the walls, first."

"That does seem a good idea." She sipped her drink and looked around. "Don't put up too many."

"I'll keep it in mind. So far I've managed a bedroom, a bath, a kitchen and a lot of scraps of paper with possibilities for the rest."

She looked around the big shadowy room and shook her head in amazement. "I gathered you weren't on the farm, but I never imagined—"

"There comes a time, Debbie darling, when a man is too old to live with his mother." He sat down on the couch beside her, the cognac glass cupped in his palm. His other arm stretched across the back of the couch, and his hand rested gently on her shoulder, warming the soft cotton under his fingertips.

It was an almost automatic gesture, Deborah thought, as if he never sat down here at all without a female companion. Well, if what she'd seen just this evening was any indication, he had no lack of opportunities with his own employees.

"I still think we should tell your mother," she said.

"Why?"

"Because. Oh, I suppose it's because I don't care if Aunt Ida thinks I'm a blithering idiot when it comes to weddings, but I don't want to have your mother thinking I'm such a fool.''

Riley frowned. His fingers began to toy with a long, glossy strand of her hair. ''Then why not just scale down the plans? Ten bridesmaids does sound a bit excessive.''

''Don't you have any sense at all, Riley? The bigger the wedding the longer it will take to plan. Therefore the less suspicion there will be when we aren't making much progress on actually committing ourselves to things like a time and a date, much less a photographer and a florist and an orchestra—''

''Orchestra? As in symphony? A band isn't good enough?''

''You know what I mean. Besides, the more expensive the wedding, the more cash Ida is going to have to come up with from the trust to pay for it, and—''

His face cleared. ''And therefore, the less she can spend on Paradise Valley.''

''Congratulations!'' Deborah said with heavy irony. ''You may go to the head of the class!''

Instead, his fingertips moved to the nape of her neck and began to massage. ''What did you and Ida find to talk about this afternoon?''

''What do you expect? You, of course. She started off by saying, 'So that's what's been taking Riley to Chicago so often. How many times has he been there lately?' and then she looked at me expectantly. And if you don't believe that called for some quick thinking, when I had no idea you'd been anywhere around! What *has* been bringing you to the big city, by the way?''

''I told you that a long time ago. Research.''

Deborah groaned.

''So what did you tell her?''

"I fluttered my eyelashes, like this, and said, 'Not nearly often enough.'"

Riley laughed. "I knew my faith in my coconspirator was justified. But the eyelashes—" he shook his head "—need a little work."

"I'm gratified to know that. Batting my eyelashes is not my favorite pastime."

"Practice. You might learn to enjoy it. And as long as we're practicing things..." His hand dropped to her spine, just between her shoulder blades, and urged her toward him, very gently.

She didn't resist, but she couldn't help saying, "I thought you had faith in your coconspirator."

"I do."

"Believe me, I already know how to conduct myself when I'm being kissed, Riley."

"I haven't a single doubt of that. Still, there are things I'd rather find out in private, like whether you enjoy being kissed on the nape of the neck, or if you slug anybody who tries."

His mouth was warm and invitingly soft against hers for a long moment, and then his lips stole softly across the hollow of her cheek to her temple.

"That is not the nape of my neck," she said, trying to sound firm.

"So I'll get around to it." It was only a husky whisper. "I think Ida could reasonably expect me to know these things, too."

She let a hint of laughter creep into her voice. "Ida probably thinks there isn't much you don't already know about me. All the time we've been together in Chicago, you know."

His mouth slipped down over her ear to the side of her neck, and then to the tiny hollow at the base of her throat, where he lingered, his tongue flicking softly at the pulse point there.

Her head had fallen back against the overstuffed couch.

After a long moment, he raised his head. "Does that mean she isn't expecting you to come home tonight?"

"Well, she didn't offer me a key." She opened her eyes with an effort. "And don't think I'm suggesting I stay here, because I'm not."

"Of course you aren't." It was soft and sultry. "You weren't invited."

She didn't mind having the nape of her neck kissed. She also didn't mind having her earlobe nibbled. And she positively enjoyed the brush of his long eyelashes against her cheek as he traced the line of her jaw with his tongue.

"You're right," he said finally. He stood up, shook his head a bit, started to refill their cognac glasses and then firmly set down the bottle as if something had changed his mind.

"What?" Deborah asked faintly.

"You do know how to conduct yourself in a kiss. R. Bristol the fifth should open a school. I think I'll call him up and suggest it."

"That's—" She bit her tongue.

Riley gave her a crooked grin. "Not a compliment? But I assure you, Debbie darling, I meant it to be one."

"I think it's time for me to go home," she said firmly.

"Before you get into trouble?"

"No. Before everybody at Lassiter House goes to bed. I'd hate to get Henry up to unlock the door. I'd never hear the last of it." *You're babbling, Deborah,* she told herself, but she went right on anyway. "Ida seems to think I only came to Summerset to be a nuisance to him, anyway. And if Preston was the one to answer the door instead . . ."

"I noticed that he seemed to find you irresistible."

"If you'd told me what sort he was, I wouldn't have bothered dragging you into this whole mess. I'd merely have gone after him."

"That would have been interesting—"

"Interesting is hardly the word."

"—watching him try to decide if he'd rather con the money from Ida or marry you for it."

Deborah gathered herself up and smoothed her skirt. "And what makes you think it's only the money he'd be after?"

Riley snorted. "Debbie, darling, do you think he's seriously interested in anything else?"

She gave him a sweet smile. "Perhaps he, too, likes the way I kiss!"

HER JAGUAR was tucked into the shadows behind the building, almost out of sight. She held out her hand for the keys, but instead Riley unlocked the passenger door and held it for her. She stood her ground. "I can get myself home, you know."

"But that would scarcely be gentlemanly of me, would it?"

She gave up and got into the car. "It's not my problem if you want to make trouble for yourself," she pointed out. "But the car stays at Lassiter House, so you're on your own when it's time to go home."

He looked up at the moon, riding high in the summer sky. "It's a lovely night for a walk," he murmured. "The moon and the clouds and the soft breeze, and the memory of the girl I love."

"Only one girl? You amaze me, Riley."

"Well, only one at a time," he amended with a smile.

"It would be only fair for you to tell me about the last few. Like the hostess at the restaurant. And the waitress."

"Ruth?" He sounded honestly amazed. "You must be joking."

A man's blind spots were uniquely interesting, Deborah thought wryly. "Then I don't suppose you noticed that Preston Powell found her intriguing."

"No, I didn't," Riley said slowly.

"I'd be careful, Riley. He may steal her affections away from you."

"What have I got to worry about?" The teasing note was back in his voice. "I've got you!"

There was no getting ahead of him, so she stopped trying. "As long as we're talking of things we should know about each other..."

"Yes, Debbie darling?" he asked solicitously.

She bit her tongue. "This ring," she said. "I'm morally certain I ought to know where it came from, and I don't."

Riley shrugged. "There's no reason you should recognize it, actually. It was my grandmother's, but she hardly ever wore it. There was too much physical work on the farm, and she didn't like to take a chance of losing it."

In the glow of a streetlight as the Jaguar flashed by, the diamond chip sparkled faintly. "Owned by a little old lady who only wore it to church on Sundays," Deborah mused.

"That's about it. It even still has the engraving inside—her initials, and my grandfather's, and something suitably soupy and sentimental. Does it fit?"

"It's a little snug, but it will do for a few days."

"I can have it adjusted."

"Oh, no. I'll be less likely to lose it this way."

Riley shrugged. "Whatever you like."

"And in any case I wouldn't want to harm it." She turned her hand. It was such a tiny stone, in such a cheap little ring. And yet, to Riley's grandmother, it had obviously been very valuable, treasured and cherished and handed down to her only grandson for his bride. For a moment, Deborah was a bit surprised that he had trusted her with it, and then she realized that he could have done nothing else without causing family speculation. "I'll be very careful with it, Riley," she said. Her voice was a little husky.

He walked her to the front door of Lassiter House. "Just in case anyone's watching," he murmured, and kissed her good-night, long and lovingly. Deborah was too breathless from the walk up the hill to protest.

And she didn't realize until she was in her own room, with the lights out and the crisp linen sheets around her, that they still hadn't formed any precise plan for how to stop Preston Powell.

CHAPTER FIVE

THE EARLY-MORNING sunshine pouring through the guest room windows had never bothered Deborah when she was a child. "But in those days," she told herself owlishly, as she pulled the blanket over her head, "Aunt Ida always sent me to bed straight after supper, so I suppose I was more than ready for a new day to come."

It was too close under the blanket to breathe, and in any case the pseudodarkness didn't do any good. There were too many arguments going on in her brain to let her rest. So she put on pastel shorts and a matching striped shirt and searched out Henry in the kitchen to beg a cup of coffee.

"It's left from breakfast, Miss Deborah," he warned. "If you don't mind waiting a bit, I'll make some fresh."

"This will be fine, Henry." Deborah poured herself a cup and stared at it for a long time. It was very black. "What time was breakfast?" she asked doubtfully.

"About two hours ago. Miss Ida's gone to the garden, and Mr. Powell went to play golf."

It begins to sound as if the man doesn't do anything else, Deborah thought uncharitably. Then she reminded herself that it was Saturday, and a good many of Preston Powell's prospects would be spending the day at the country club. It would be an opportunity he couldn't afford to miss. She pulled a chair over to the heavy, knife-scarred table that served as a butcher block and island in the center of the big old-fashioned room. "How long has Preston Powell been living here, Henry?"

"About three weeks, miss."

"He's put all this together in three weeks? The whole Paradise Valley project, I mean."

"Oh, no. He's been doing that for some months, I understand. I thought you meant how long he'd been at Lassiter House."

Deborah sipped her coffee and tried not to make a face. "Ida's put up with him for that long? You don't like him any better than I do, do you, Henry?"

"It's not my job to like him or not," the houseman said primly. He took his hands out of the dishwater and began to dry his fingers carefully, one at a time. "Now if you'll excuse me, I have to answer the telephone."

"Never mind. I'll get it." She left her coffee on the kitchen table without regret and dashed through the butler's pantry to the tiny telephone booth in the side hall. In Jacob Lassiter's day, one telephone was a luxury; more than that would have been scandalous, despite his standing in the community. And what was good enough for him had remained good enough for his family. Ida hadn't even installed an extension in her bedroom until she fell one winter, broke her leg and was confined to her room for weeks.

"Hello, Deborah darling!" William Ainsley sounded extraordinarily cheerful. "I have good news, I think."

She relaxed. "Hi, Daddy."

"I found my copy of the trust arrangement. Shall I send you— Oh, darling, I should have asked. Can you talk? If someone is listening in, just say 'bananas' and I'll understand."

Deborah laughed, but she looked over her shoulder before she said, "Daddy, this is not a CIA stakeout, for heaven's sake. Of course I can talk."

"Oh, good. I haven't forgotten what it's like in Ida's house. When I was visiting her I tried a time or two to call my broker, and she always walked through the hall at the wrong time. She seemed to think I was placing bets with a bookie or arranging an assignation with a hooker—"

"Oh, was her hearing going even then?" Deborah asked cheerfully.

"Just remember, dear, 'bananas,' and I'll know what you mean. I'll send you a copy of the trust document."

She shifted her grip on the telephone. "How about giving me a rundown of the relevant parts now?"

"Let me see." She could imagine him arranging his half glasses on the bridge of his nose, and she could hear the rustling of paper. "As for money for the wedding—"

"Daddy, that is hardly my biggest concern at the moment."

"Of course not. Silly of me. The original trustees were Jacob's three children, Ralph and Ida and your grandmother. Now, of course, there's only Ida, and Riley is right—she's got total control. After her death, control passes to..." He flipped a page, and the telephone rattled as he almost dropped it. "To the trust department of Jacob's bank and to the senior partner of his law firm, jointly."

Deborah groaned. "And trying to get information out of either of them, or for that matter to get them involved in unseating Aunt Ida, will be impossible."

"Very likely."

"Wait a minute. What does he mean, the senior partner of his law firm? The one who handled his business? If he was Jacob's age, he'd be at least a hundred years old by now.''

"It isn't terribly clear, but I suppose it means whoever is the senior partner at the moment. Law firms tend to go on and on, you know, they just change personnel over the years.''

"Too bad Riley didn't make it through law school,'' Deborah said grumpily. ''It might have been him, and he could have fought this battle all by himself.''

William Ainsley made a noise that might have been agreement. ''The firm's name at the time was Bowers and Milligan.''

Deborah riffled through the telephone directory. ''Well, there's no Bowers in Summerset now,'' she reported. ''And no Milligan, either.''

"Well, I'll send this to you. Maybe you and Riley can make something more of it than I have. Good luck, darling.''

"Daddy, maybe you'd better send it to Riley. I'd hate to have it opened by mistake here at Lassiter House.''

"So there is some spying going on, after all.'' There was satisfaction in William's tone. ''As long as we're talking about intrigue, I stopped at the gallery yesterday to see how things were going in your absence, just to make sure there was no funny business.''

"I'd only been gone a few hours,'' Deborah said dryly. ''How bad could it have gotten?''

"You never know. That assistant of yours—Peggy, is that her name? She's very good, Deborah.''

"Daddy,'' she said wistfully, ''please don't tell me Peggy sold you something.''

"Only a small watercolor.''

"Oh, is that all? You traitor!''

"Well, if I'd waited for you to come back, someone else might have got it," William Ainsley said reasonably. "I'll talk to you later, darling. Shall we set up a regular call schedule, so I can notify the authorities if I don't hear from you?"

IDA WAS TRIMMING the faded blooms off the old-fashioned roses in the walled garden behind the house. The huge old plants clambered up the walls, clinging tenaciously to the brick and mortar. Deborah wondered how badly scratched little Alec had been in his first few expeditions to the forbidden swimming pool. Had he come upon the hidden roses without warning, having climbed the wall and dropped into them? And how long, she wondered, had it taken him to pinpoint the safest spots for scaling the barricade? Not long, she suspected, remembering the beach ball ploy; Alec had a very well-developed sense of self-preservation.

"Good morning, Aunt Ida," she called from the French doors, and was annoyed when Ida glanced at the position of the sun before answering.

It's not all that late, Deborah told herself. *In Chicago I'd only be starting for the gallery.* But she swallowed her annoyance and circled the pool slowly to join her aunt. "May I help?"

Ida shook her head. "It's touchy, pruning these old plants."

"I thought I could learn."

Aunt Ida shot her a look. "Don't tell me you're bored with Summerset already."

"Of course not. I just haven't anything else to do at the moment."

"Riley hasn't offered to put you to work? I'm surprised at the boy, passing up a chance for free help."

Riley has better sense than to try, Deborah thought. She sat down on the edge of a stone bench. "I suppose that comes later. He's picking me up in a few minutes, by the way. We're spending the day out at the farm."

"I gathered that. It's lucky he can take time off whenever he wants like that. I'd think it would concern him, leaving the hired help in charge."

"Aunt Ida, no one should work all the time. And if he's got good hired help..." Deborah pulled her heels up on the edge of the bench and hugged her knees. Then she added deliberately, "I thought you liked Riley."

Ida's pruning shears didn't pause. "And who said I didn't?"

"You certainly sounded yesterday as if you didn't approve."

"Of Riley?" Ida sounded more curious than surprised.

"Of our plans." Deborah bit her tongue and forced herself to actually say the words. "The whole idea of us getting married."

Ida turned around then, and it seemed to Deborah that there was nothing but honest amazement behind her old-fashioned wire eyeglasses. "That sounds a bit guilty, Deborah. I wonder why. Do you know of some reason why I shouldn't approve? Something you haven't told me?"

So much for the direct approach, Deborah thought. She shrugged. "Of course not. I just got that impression from you. Of course, Riley is a bit unorthodox." She congratulated herself; if that understatement didn't sound like a woman in love, nothing ever would!

"Yes," Ida said thoughtfully. "I must admit I was surprised."

"I thought perhaps you might be upset at the idea of me living in a warehouse, or something."

Ida had gone back to trimming the roses. "At least it's a *converted* warehouse," she pointed out. "And why should I care where you live? Just don't get any notions of living here."

Deborah stifled a shudder at the idea of Lassiter House as a honeymoon cottage. The mere suggestion of being part of a newlywed couple sharing that monstrosity on the hill with Aunt Ida made her feel ill. She said with perfect honesty, "The idea had never crossed my mind."

"Good. I'm putting it up for sale, you know."

"Lassiter House?" It was almost a croak. Lassiter House without Aunt Ida? No, this must be a colossal joke.

"It's too big," Ida went on, "and Henry's getting too old to keep up with it."

"You could hire more help," Deborah offered tentatively.

Ida shook her head decisively. "That would be a waste of money. As soon as it sells, I'm going to build a small place out at Preston's resort. I've already got my site picked out."

Deborah's uneasiness faded a bit. At least Ida was being sensible enough to wait for her house to sell before plunging into something new, and a sale could take months or years, or forever. Who would be fool enough to buy Lassiter House, anyway?

It's a dinosaur of a house, she told herself. *It hasn't had an ounce of updating in the forty years since Jacob died. There's still no air-conditioning, the plumbing is beginning to be balky, and the kitchen could have come straight out of* Wuthering Heights. *Who would want the place?*

It was with considerably more calmness that she said, "You're right. A smaller place would be much easier for you to manage, Aunt Ida."

Ida sniffed. "I can manage anything I choose. It's Henry I'm worried about. Besides, it's only sensible to keep an eye on my investment."

Deborah swallowed hard and told herself that there would be no advantage in arguing with Aunt Ida about Paradise Valley. Not just yet, at any rate.

Ida was watching her curiously. "You don't approve of the resort, do you?"

"That's not up to me," Deborah said steadily. *Now I'm beginning to sound like Henry,* she thought. "I'm certain that you'll look into it very carefully before you actually make any big investment. Especially with the trust's money, knowing as you do how determined your father was to keep his estate intact."

"And also because of the expense of your wedding coming up?" Aunt Ida asked mildly.

"I didn't say that. But as long as we're on the subject, perhaps you'll tell me if there is anything I should know before I start making plans."

"You mean if there are limits, or things you're not allowed to buy, and that sort of thing? No, there aren't—not really. I think sometimes that my father had no sense at all."

At least we agree on something, Deborah thought wryly. *Personally, I'm beginning to think the man was a certifiable nut! Perhaps old Jacob wasn't so big on the idea of marriage after all. He must have managed to take all the joy out of weddings by making them into family fights.*

Then she thought once more about what Ida had said, and asked suspiciously, "Exactly what do you mean, *not really?*"

Aunt Ida smiled. Her procelain-perfect teeth gleamed between the thin lips. "I have to approve all of the bills," she said gently.

"I expect that you'll look them over very carefully," Deborah said calmly. *Thank heaven it isn't going to come to that,* she thought. *I wonder how Mother managed. But then she didn't have Paradise Valley and Preston Powell to contend with!* "I'd hate to think I wasn't getting my money's worth."

"Or—to be painfully accurate, my father's money's worth," Ida agreed.

Before Deborah could get her breath back again after that jab, Ida went on, "Your mother had a small but very pretty wedding. Of course, your Uncle Ralph had a few things to say about that."

I suppose, Deborah thought, *that means Ralph stood up to Ida, and took Vivien's part.*

"And so we had to fight for everything," Ida mused. "This time it will be much easier. Do you know he didn't think that orchids were reasonable at all? Your poor mother had to settle for roses. And you should have heard the fuss he kicked up about the champagne. He actually thought it didn't need to be vintage or French—or even champagne at all!"

Deborah put out her hand experimentally, resting it against the warm brick wall. No, she was still upright on the bench. She hadn't fallen and hit her head against the tiles and concrete; for a moment she had thought that was the only explanation of the sounds she was hearing. It certainly sounded like Ida's voice, going on about taffeta and alençon lace and ice sculptures and a wedding breakfast that sounded like food for the gods....

She's flipped, Deborah told herself in astonishment. *Yesterday she looked sour at the mere mention of Riley's name. Today...!*

"Aunt Ida," she said. It was little more than a croak.

Ida stopped pruning and looked quizzically at Deborah. "Didn't anyone ever tell you?" she asked. "It's foolishly sentimental of me, I suppose, but I've always been crazy about weddings."

It was like biting into a bit of rare beefsteak and finding herself with a mouthful of marshmallow cream. Deborah almost choked on the taste of it.

"I'm glad you're going to be married here in Summerset so I can really be involved," Ida went on gently. "It will be fun to give you a wedding no one will ever forget. That reminds me—we'll have to talk to Father Adams right away and reserve the church. I'll call him and make an appointment for tomorrow after early services."

It took a moment for Deborah to find words. In the meantime, Ida continued to murmur happily to herself about the relative merits of limousines versus horse-drawn carriages; of white cake, chocolate cake, fruit cake or a many-tiered combination of all three; and of satin caps as opposed to flowers for holding a veil in place.

"You are going to wear a veil, aren't you, Deborah?" she asked anxiously. "It's hardly a wedding without one, but . . . well, you are eligible for one still, aren't you?"

Deborah, who had just cleared her throat, lost her power of speech again over that one. The idea of Aunt Ida matter-of-factly inquiring if she was still a virgin and therefore entitled to the symbolic veil . . .

Behind her, a husky voice said, "Of course she's going to wear a veil. I have dreams about Debbie in a veil." Riley's arms went around her and Deborah screamed weakly as he lifted her clear off the bench in an enthusiastic bear hug.

Ida's look of half-abstracted concern faded into something like genuine amusement. "What a lucky girl you are, dear," she murmured.

Riley let Deborah slide back to the ground, still holding her tightly against him, and pressed his lips to the side of her throat. "Yes, you are," he whispered. "A very lucky girl, that I came along just in time to stop that kind of question."

"Have a good time at the farm, children," Ida said with a dismissing wave of a gloved hand. "I suppose your mother is still being stubborn about poor Preston, Riley?"

"I wouldn't put it quite that way," Riley replied evasively.

"No, I'm sure you wouldn't. You're missing a wonderful opportunity yourself, you know. You really should make an investment for your future. I'm sure Preston would be happy to talk to you about the possibilities."

"I'm sure he would," Riley agreed. "But unfortunately, until I've married my heiress I don't have anything to invest." The smile he directed at Deborah was a kindly one.

Ida laughed. It was almost a girlish giggle.

They were halfway down the hill to his car when Riley asked casually, "By the way, can you wear a veil?"

Deborah's voice was pure ice. "What possible business is it of yours?"

"Oh, mere curiosity," he said cheerfully. "And a little ammunition for the next time we schedule a fight about the wedding plans. You can hardly have ten bridesmaids if you can't wear the established costume yourself. The symbol of innocence and purity and all that."

She wanted to kick him. "You busybody! You wouldn't dare bring that up in a public fight."

He looked thoughtful. "Probably only the final, climactic one."

"Well, if you aren't more careful about what you say, you aren't going to need the final, climactic fight, because you'll have messed things up long before that. You might as well have told Aunt Ida straight out just now that you're only marrying me for my money. Talk about asking for trouble, Riley.''

"All the best dynastic alliances involve money," he said earnestly. "But in any case, she didn't believe me.''

"Oh, really?"

"Really. And she shouldn't believe it, either, because no amount of money would be enough to make me marry you," he added blithely.

Deborah's anger deflated abruptly, like a punctured balloon. She thought about refusing to go with him at all, and stalking back to the house, but there was that hill, and Aunt Ida, who was probably writing the wedding vows by now. All in all, she'd rather put up with Riley. So she trailed along after him, still a bit bemused.

Riley said, as if he'd just noticed, "Why are you wearing pink shorts? Have you forgotten we're going to the farm?"

"I've outgrown my mud puddle days, thank you," Deborah told him grandly. "Unless you plan to put me to work stacking hay bales, I don't expect to have any trouble staying clean.''

"No more hay. Just zucchini and cucumbers and tomatoes and cabbage and brussels sprouts and—" He interrupted himself as they sped through downtown. "Would you mind awfully if I bring someone else along?"

Deborah shrugged. "It's your party."

"He doesn't get a chance to get out in the country much, and his mother's working today."

A child, and obviously not one of Mary Beth's. *It was silly of you, Deborah,* she told herself, *to assume that it would be female, and not a child.* She had suspected he meant that gorgeous blond hostess of his, and now she poked fun at herself for the very idea.

But it did startle her when they stopped in front of a small bungalow at the edge of the business district and a boy came racing across the lawn toward the car.

"It's Ruth's kid," Riley said. He sounded a little defensive. "And don't give me that I-told-you-so look, either. He's a friend of mine and his mother's a good worker and they're having a tough time—"

"And you're only trying to help out," Deborah finished. "Good intentions get more people in trouble than any other thing in the world. Hi, Alec."

The child's eyes rounded. "You're Riley's girl?"

Riley muttered, "I should have known you two would have met already. May I ask where?"

"You may not," Deborah said briefly.

It didn't take much of an invitation to persuade Alec to join them, but it did require a direct order from Riley to make him return to the house long enough to leave a note for his mother. Then he piled into the back of the car. He poked his head over the seat between them and began a nonstop monologue that lasted till they were well out of town.

Finally Deborah interrupted firmly. "Let's drive through Paradise Valley on the way."

"Why?"

"Because how am I supposed to be a detective without seeing the scene of the crime? Honestly, Riley, don't you ever read mysteries?"

"Crime?" Alec asked. "You mean like murder?"

"Now you've torn it," Riley muttered. "Deborah was speaking figuratively, Alec, which is just another way of saying she was making it up."

Alec looked disappointed.

"It will only take a minute to drive through," Deborah argued.

Riley shook his head. "We'd have to hike in. The snake put in a new security fence and gate so no one can drive in anymore."

"I wonder why."

"Use your head, Deb," he said irritably. "He doesn't want visitors running around loose, poking into things. He wants to be on hand to do a sales pitch for every one of them. That's not the reason he gives, of course. He says it's a matter of liability insurance. Now that he's responsible for the place, he doesn't want anyone drowning without his permission. Are you up for a walk?"

Deborah held up one foot, in a sturdy walking shoe. "You're talking to someone who does miles every day on concrete."

"Not the same thing at all." Riley glanced at his watch. "We could come later this afternoon," he said. "It will take some time."

Alec's head popped up again from the back seat. "I want to go, too," he chimed in. "Mom and I are going to get rich from Paradise Valley, you know."

Deborah's gaze locked with Riley's for what seemed eternity. It could only have been a split second, however; the car had not even wavered when Riley looked back at the road and said, "Really, Alec? That's interesting."

Deborah could hear the strain in his voice; she didn't think Alec was likely to pick it up.

"Heck, yes," Alec said. "She told me it's a lot better than just leaving the money in the bank. Dad's insurance money, I mean," he added unnecessarily.

Deborah closed her eyes in pain, remembering Ruth's thin, eager face, the efficient way she had gone about her job—and the way Preston Powell had flirted with her last night. "Widows and children," she said under her breath. "Is there anything the man won't do?"

Nothing more was said, but neither was there any doubt about whether they were going to stop at Paradise Valley.

The resort lay several miles west of the city, in a natural hollow. Local legend had it that Paradise Lake, fed by the Summer River, had been originally formed by beavers, generations before the first human settlers had seen it. Now the water was trapped by a huge engineering marvel of a man-made dam, and a much larger lake was the proud centerpiece of an Eden of opportunity for vacationers.

Except that here, as in that other Eden, humanity was no longer to be found on any regular basis.

Riley parked the car on the shoulder of the road just out of sight from the shiny new steel security gates, and they climbed through a ditch full of brush and weeds and random stale puddles—and probably poison ivy, Deborah thought—wriggled through the barbed-wire fence, and were inside.

A shell of a building near the entrance, a guard shack with a fallen-in roof, a great many twisting ribbons of concrete leading nowhere in particular and a filling station with gasoline pumps frozen at a ten-year-old price were all that remained of the original attempt to build a resort.

"It's like a concentration camp in here," Deborah muttered.

But once the fence was left behind, that impression dissipated. The whole resort looked faded and unkempt, as if it needed a good scrubbing. But it was easy to see what the plan had been.

"The streets look as if they're in pretty good shape," Deborah said, trying her best to be fair.

"Yes, they do—but I wouldn't care to vouch for the sewers and water mains and natural gas lines that run underneath."

"Oh. I hadn't thought of that." She scuffed the toe of her shoe against a curb lined with weeds. She itched to pull them out. "He could at least hire someone to neaten up the place."

"He did, when he first came to town," Riley said somberly. "If he was serious, he would keep it up."

"Well, I see why Preston wants to give the tours himself. So he can put the best possible explanations on everything. Keep people from asking too many questions."

"He does a good job of it, too. Over there the plans call for a five-hundred-room hotel." Riley made a sweeping gesture.

Deborah whistled faintly.

"And in this section there's room for about three hundred summer cottages. I'm using the term *cottages* lightly, because one of the conditions on the purchase of a lot is to set a minimum price for the house that's built on it."

"It's sizable, I suppose?" Deborah hazarded.

"You probably wouldn't think so, compared to Chicago—considering what you must have paid for your apartment. But let's just say there were only a half dozen houses in that price range sold last year in all of Summerset."

"And he thinks people will build three hundred of them here?" Deborah added thoughtfully, "I wonder where Aunt Ida's lot is."

"She has one?"

"I thought you knew everything," she said sweetly. "Hasn't the grapevine told you that she's selling Lassiter House?"

"You're joking."

"No, I'm not. But I agree. Aunt Ida without Lassiter House is unthinkable. It's like bagels without cream cheese."

"Or Laurel without Hardy," Riley agreed.

"Peanut butter without jelly."

"I've got it. Politics without corruption!"

"I think you've missed the point, Riley. I wasn't playing a new game." She frowned.

Alec had run down the long slope to the lake. "Do you suppose we'd better go after him?" Riley asked.

Deborah nodded, and said absently, "When that boy gets around water he shows no sense at all. I'm afraid to ask...is it still a real lake? Or has it all silted in and it's only a mirage now?"

"Last time I checked, it was still deep enough to swim in. However, the beaches..."

From the top of the gentle hill, Paradise Lake itself was still the shining blue basin that Deborah remembered. But as they drew nearer she saw what Riley's unfinished sentence meant. The sandy beaches were only ghosts of their former inviting selves; one had grown up knee-high in weeds, another had been washed almost entirely away by seasons of heavy rain.

Alec was standing in the middle of the weeds, his face woebegone. Deborah could see the disappointment in the set of his shoulders; she could almost feel it radiating from him. She wanted to put her arms around him and tell him everything would be all right.

But she couldn't, because she was so terribly afraid it wouldn't be all right at all. Not for Alec, and not for Ruth, and not for any of the people of Summerset who had trusted their futures to a man like Preston Powell.

CHAPTER SIX

DEBORAH WANTED to cry, or else go straight back to Summerset and commit assault and battery on Preston Powell. Instead she took out her frustration by pulling up a weed at her feet, and then eyed its deep, well-established root system with astonishment. It had left a gaping hole in the sand.

"The beach would have to be torn out, of course," Riley said meditatively. He was standing with feet planted firmly in the sand, his hands on his hips, looking at the expanse of weeds.

"The whole place needs to be redone," Deborah muttered. "It would be cheaper to start over somewhere else if you were really serious about a resort."

"Oh, it's probably not quite that bad. There's no sense in throwing out all the basic, expensive work that's been done—the streets, the utilities, the surveying."

"I thought you said you wouldn't vouch for the utilities."

"I wouldn't. Still, almost any amount of repairs would be less expensive than starting from scratch. Take the golf course, for instance. It was constructed last time around." He waved a hand at a rolling hill on the other side of the lake. "Of course it would take a whole lot of work to get it back into shape, but it's all still out there under the brush."

"And there's plenty of brush," Deborah said a bit sourly as she waded through the overgrowth on the walk back to the car. Her unprotected shins felt as if they'd been sandpapered. "It's astounding," she added. "The size of the project. It doesn't make any logical sense at all."

Riley shrugged. "Since he's not going to actually build anything, why shouldn't he plan on a grand scale? Drawing lines on paper is cheap."

"But why is everyone falling for it? How can anyone look at this mess and actually believe that the project will come to anything, when he can't even get the weeds pulled?"

"Would you invest your life savings in a ten-unit hotel? Doesn't a five-hundred-room one sound a lot more stable and secure?"

"Neither one of them sounds exactly inviting to me," she said frankly. "I'm not big on taking financial risks, anyway."

Riley snorted. "You? As if starting a gallery in a city that already has five hundred isn't taking a risk!"

"That's different," she said. "I'm not exactly investing in old masters. I buy what I know and believe in, and I know when to ask for advice."

"Great," Riley groaned. "By that rule of thumb, Ida and Ruth are doing exactly the right thing!"

"And I'm not risking my daily bread and butter," she added morosely. "Though if Aunt Ida has her way, I'll have to."

Riley looked at her sharply, but he didn't comment.

Alec said, in a voice that just escaped being a whine, "I thought there would be a float to swim out to. And a playground. The pictures had a playground!"

It didn't take much imagination to know what he meant, even though Deborah hadn't seen the promotional brochures herself. She wondered if Alec's mother knew any more about Paradise Valley than the child did, or if her investment had been made solely on the basis of those slick promotional brochures.

DEBORAH HAD NOT FORGOTTEN the approach to Anna Maria Lassiter's farm, a long curving lane that led down a gently sloping hill to the buildings set well back from the road. Even though she knew it was no longer a grain farm, her memory had painted a cornfield framing the big white house, and it was almost a shock to see a neatly tended patchwork of vegetable gardens stretching as far as she could see, instead of the waving sea of shoulder-high green stalks.

The lawn seemed full of people. A couple of tow-headed children ran toward the car. One of them, a girl just old enough to have lost both her front teeth, was calling, "Uncle Riley!"

Mary Beth's kids, Deborah thought. *The boy must be her big brother. I didn't realize they'd have grown up so much. And I don't even remember their names.*

Deborah's gaze happened to be on the girl's face at the moment she saw Alec. Distaste dawned in the child's wide blue eyes, and she cast a scathing look at Riley as if to ask how he could do this to her. Deborah had to bite her lip to keep from smiling at the memories it evoked.

I must have looked just like that, she thought, *when I was seven years old and my eyes fell unexpectedly on Riley! Not that things have changed so much, actually.*

Alec seemed to have forgotten his disappointment at the lake. "Zach!" he called with delight, and the boys went tearing off toward the barns. Deborah thought she heard something about a bird's nest Zach had discovered.

Obviously Riley had heard it, too. "There isn't a bird within a mile who's safe with those two around," he muttered, and swung the girl up into his arms. "Especially this one. How's my Robin?"

"Why did you have to bring Alec?" she asked.

"You're just like your mother, aren't you?" Riley asked. "Straight to the point and no nonsense. Give me the benefit of the doubt, won't you? At least Alec took Zach off and now neither of them is teasing you."

Robin tossed her head.

"Did I heard you talking about me again, Riley? Hello, Deborah—welcome home." Mary Beth disentangled herself from the blond child on her lap and held out her hand.

Riley had been right, Deborah thought. Mary Beth was no longer the lithe beauty she remembered. Matronly, that was the word for her now. She looked prosperous and sleek and well groomed and contented in her white skirt and red blouse.

"Where have you been?" she went on. "This is a bad habit, Riley, never being on time. I'm sure you've discovered already, Deborah, that something always conspires to make him late. In fact, you might want to tell Riley the wedding is half an hour before it really is."

Riley gave his sister a slow, lazy grin. "Debbie would wait for me forever, wouldn't you, darling?"

"With pleasure," Deborah returned gently. In fact, she wanted to add, the longer the wait, the better! It reminded her that she hadn't yet told him about Aunt Ida's enthusiastic plans. And she hadn't asked him about that law firm, either.

But there was no chance, then. Anna Maria had set up a picnic on the lawn, and she seemed to have invited half the county. Deborah scarcely got a chance to eat because of the continual procession of well-wishers.

But she couldn't help overhearing when the owner of a nearby farm asked Anna Maria when she was going to be sensible about her land, and whether it was fair to hold out for more than her neighbors had gotten. And a moment later, Mary Beth chimed in, "Mother, why don't you sell? Rod and I both think you're being foolish to pass up this wonderful opportunity, you know. You and Alan could retire and take it easy for a change, instead of slaving out here."

"And what would we live on?" Anna Maria asked absently, as if she had been through this discussion so many times she no longer had to think about it at all. "It's hard to spend stock certificates at the supermarket, that's sure. Boys, stop tormenting Robin and finish cranking the ice cream freezer."

Deborah had lost her appetite. She felt like a small boat adrift in a foggy harbor, unsure what direction to steer next but dead sure that if she didn't do something she was going to be run down by a freighter named Preston Powell.

She spotted Riley across the lawn, perched on top of the split-rail fence. He smiled at her, and the warm reassurance of that gesture made her put her plate aside and go over to him.

It's silly, she thought, *but at least I know where I stand with him. I'm not sure about anyone else.*

He reached for her hand and drew her close to him till she was leaning against the fence, her shoulder brushing his chest. She was slightly off balance, and so she put her arm around him to steady herself. He continued his conversation without a break while his fingertips drew patterns on the soft skin of her upper arm so idly that he seemed to have no idea that he was doing anything of the kind. The touch tickled, and every breath he released stirred her hair, and the soft resonance of his voice seemed to vibrate through her bones.

I'll bet, she thought idly, *that if I tipped my head back, I'd be at just the right angle to steal a kiss...*

It was an unsettling sort of sensation, as if the earth below her feet had suddenly turned to quivering gelatin. She shivered a little. *And why would you want to steal a kiss?* she asked herself sternly. *Don't get caught up in your own one act play, Deborah, my girl.*

Riley asked softly, "Shall we go for a walk?"

The matron he'd been talking to smiled knowingly. It annoyed Deborah a bit, but she did want to talk to him, so she nodded.

He jumped down from the fence and interlaced his fingers with Deborah's. "I'll take you down by the creek," he told her. "It's quiet there."

The route took them past a huge field of tomato vines, heavy with ripening fruit, and down a winding path to a rippling brook, its banks almost lined with trees and bushes and berry brambles. In one spot, however, the grassy meadow dipped almost to the water, and it was here that Riley stopped and dropped to the ground to sit cross-legged in the sun. "What's on your mind?" he asked bluntly.

Deborah shrugged. "I've said I'll try to help, but I don't even know where to begin," she said hopelessly. "I'm an outsider. No one's going to listen to me. And everybody seems to be sold on the idea, anyway." She pulled up her heels and hugged her knees tightly and didn't look at him as she said, "Riley, is it possible that *we're* the ones who are wrong? Maybe we're the ones who are prejudiced, or paranoid. It could be a good investment after all."

Riley sighed and threw himself back against the grass, full-length. "Not you, too."

"Not really," she admitted. "Personally, I wouldn't trust Preston Powell enough to invest a subway token. But it's hard to be so outnumbered and still hold firm."

Riley pushed himself up on his elbows. "There's a man who used to live here, a businessman, who moved to Florida years ago," he said slowly. "He was back a couple of months ago for a visit, and when he heard the story of Paradise Valley, he went through the roof. I heard it. He was having lunch at the restaurant, and I happened to be seating a party at the next table. It seems he'd heard of Preston Powell before, in connection with an elaborate resort in the Everglades."

"One that went bankrupt and drained all the investors' money?" Deborah speculated.

"You've got it."

She glared at him. "And you didn't tell me that? Dammit, Riley, you didn't have to drag me into this at all! You could have just told Aunt Ida—"

"The man's a friend of Ida's, Deborah."

No "Debbie darling," she noted idly.

"In fact," he said heavily, "it was Ida he was having lunch with."

Deborah's lips formed a soundless oh.

"I don't know what Ida had to say about it—I could scarcely stand behind her chair and eavesdrop—but I can tell you what Mary Beth's reaction was when I told her about it. She said that I shouldn't be foolish, that every venture capitalist has a failure now and then, and that he'd certainly learned from the problems in the Everglades so they wouldn't be repeated at Paradise Valley. Shall I go on?"

"No need," Deborah said glumly. "I get the picture."

"People believe what they want to believe, Deb."

She sighed. "So, it's back to the beginning, isn't it? Well, the only clue I have is that Daddy told me there was a law firm in Summerset called Bowers and Milligan that used to handle Jacob's business. Are they still around somewhere?"

Riley shrugged. "It doesn't ring a bell with me. Ask Mom, she'll know."

If I really thought it would make any difference, Deborah thought, *I'd rush back there and ask her this minute.* Instead, she stretched out beside him on the long grass. "Who is Ida's attorney now?"

"Mary Beth's husband."

"The one who thinks Paradise Valley is a great opportunity?" she said wryly.

He almost smiled. "That's the only husband she has, as far as I know. And he's a stickler for ethics, too. Nobody tries anything shady with Rod Walters."

"The irony of that simply defeats me." Deborah closed her eyes. If it weren't for the damned problem with the resort, she thought, she could have really enjoyed this. It was so peaceful out here, just the sigh of the breeze in the branches, a bird calling in the distance, the rustle of some small animal behind the big oak tree that arched above their heads. She listened to the tiny, hypnotic sounds of nature for a long time. "There used to be whippoorwills out here," she said sleepily.

"There still are, at twilight."

"Wake me up in time to hear them."

Riley warned, "You'll fry if you go to sleep out here in the open. And we were talking about Paradise Valley, anyway."

"I'm tired of Paradise Valley," Deborah said, without opening her eyes. "And I don't want to let it spoil my nap."

"All right," he said genially, and she relaxed. But when he rolled away from her and jumped up a moment later, a warning bell sounded deep inside Deborah's head.

She looked up at him warily. "You wouldn't leave me out here, would you?"

"Of course not. I'm just going for a walk down by the water." It sounded too cheerful to be real, and a moment later she knew why. "I haven't gone frog-catching for years...."

She grabbed for him as he walked away and managed to lock both her hands around his ankle. He dragged her for a couple of steps and then stopped and put his hands on his hips, looking down at her with a sparkle in his eyes.

"You don't like that idea?" he hazarded.

"Not exactly. See what you've done to my clothes? Grass stains all over them!"

"I'm not the one who turned you into a human sleigh." He dropped down beside her. "But at least it got you into the shade, so you won't burn. Would you like me to kiss you and make it better?"

"Kiss the grass stains, you mean? I hardly think—"

He obviously didn't mean the grass stains, and her protest died to a soft little sigh under the first sultry touch of his mouth against hers. He smiled and eased her back against the grass, his forearm forming a pillow for her head. The whole length of him was warm against her side, and his thumb wandered down her throat, coming to rest in the hollow at the base of it, where it stayed to magnify the jerky beat of her pulse. Almost against her will, her hand slipped to the back of his neck, and he kissed her again.

There were fragments of grass caught in his hair, and he carried the scent of sunshine and soft breezes. It was the most sensual sort of cologne she'd ever smelled.

His hand wandered over her shoulder and down her arm, and then tentatively brushed her breast. He nibbled at her lower lip, tugging at it softly with his teeth, and raised his head to smile at her.

There was something in his gaze that puzzled her a bit. Not triumph; it wasn't so cold as that. Satisfaction, perhaps—was that it? So few men seemed to enjoy this sort of caress for itself. She didn't mind admitting that she was enjoying it herself.

And that's the problem, she warned herself. *You're enjoying it too much. This is a delightful way to pass a little time, but don't forget why you're really here.*

Still, it had been an awfully long time since she had been kissed quite so enthusiastically, and she could feel the glow of lazy contentment spreading slowly through her veins.

There was a rustle in the tree above them, as if a large bird had been suddenly startled off a nest. In the same instant a girlish voice called from the top of the slope, "I see you, Zach! I'm going to tell!"

Riley turned his head just as a bright red blur dropped from the tree. Deborah screamed a wordless, futile warning just as the object struck Riley's nose and exploded with a wet gush, splashing over his face and hair and clothes. The overflow soaked her, as well.

Riley sat up and wiped his eyes with the back of his hand. Two chortling figures dropped from the tree and hit the ground running; they topped the hill with Robin staying a bare stride ahead of them, and Riley sank back against the grass. "There's no sense in chasing the little monsters," he muttered. "I'll catch up with them later, and they'll pay. Where did they get the damned water balloon, anyway?"

"And how long were they up there with it?" Deborah added.

"You might well ask. I suppose we were too absorbed to notice." He rubbed his sleeve across his face and shook drops of water from his hair as a dog would. "Shall we go on from where we were so rudely interrupted? The kids will probably have told everyone up at the house what we were doing anyway."

"We weren't doing anything so very terrible," Deborah said defensively.

"That's what I mean. We might as well enjoy ourselves. That's a very interesting new fashion twist, Debbie darling." He leaned back on one elbow and his index fingertip slid slowly from her still-dripping chin down the soaked front of her knit shirt.

She jumped up so suddenly that her head swam. "On the other hand, a hike up the ridge to see where Preston is going to put the toboggan run sounds awfully exciting."

Riley frowned and sat up. "Toboggan run? Here? Did Ida tell you that?"

"No. It just seemed like a logical next step. Maybe he's going to try to bring the Winter Olympics here."

"Please don't start talking like that in public, Deb," he said somberly. "Half the town would believe you, and the next thing you know you'd be reading it on the front page of the local paper as gospel truth."

Deborah ran her hands through her hair. "Talking of gospel truth reminds me. I hope you've got a good excuse not to go to church tomorrow."

"What? And risk my immortal soul?"

Deborah looked down at him disparagingly. "I doubt missing church once would be enough to make a difference."

He looked offended. "Are you implying I'm already in danger?"

"Well, if we lie to Father Adams—is that his name?"

Riley nodded.

"About our intentions of getting married, we'll both end up in big trouble."

"Why would we—"

"Because Aunt Ida is making an appointment for us to talk to him after the service tomorrow, that's why. Just when I thought I'd outgrown her rules about early church, she comes up with this!"

Riley thoughtfully pulled up a stalk of grass and began to chew it. "I don't like the sound of this."

"It gets worse, Riley. She's taking over the wedding plans. If we don't get out of this mess soon, Aunt Ida will have arranged for the entire Seventh Cavalry to show up and form an arch of swords outside the church on our wedding day."

"I really don't like the sound of this, Deb."

"Well, don't start blaming it on me! You're the one who announced that this supposed spectacle is coming off in Summerset, you idiot. If you'd let me have my way, Ida wouldn't have had any reason to dive into the plans. No one would have even wondered whether we were making headway!"

"All right," Riley conceded handsomely. "Perhaps I did mess up a bit on that one."

"Mess up? It looks to me as if you didn't just put your foot in your mouth, you stuck it all the way down your throat," she said grimly. "At the rate she's going she'll have spent the whole trust fund on this wedding."

"And wasted it," Riley agreed. "Because when the wedding doesn't happen, she'll have thrown away all that money for nothing."

They looked at each other in horror.

"No, she won't," he said.

Deborah sat down hard on the grass and said weakly, "Because if we don't have a wedding after all, then the trust won't pay for anything. And the question becomes, who ends up stuck with the bills?"

"It was your idea," Riley said uncompromisingly.

Deborah sighed. "The engagement, maybe. But you wouldn't have caught me dead in this town if you hadn't begged me to come down here. And that makes you half-responsible."

"You're the one with the money."

"Not for long, at this rate!"

"We could just go through with it," Riley suggested.

"The trust pays for weddings, idiot. Divorces are not included. We wouldn't gain a thing."

"Well, at least that way we wouldn't be in debt for Ida's idea of a party."

"Good. You're finally admitting you share the responsibility for this fiasco!"

There was a long silence. "I think we'd better start by following up your one clue," Riley said. "Fast."

"Good idea." She stretched up her hands to him and he obligingly lifted her to her feet, without apparent effort.

Most of the crowd had dispersed. They found Anna Maria in the kitchen drinking tea; nearby Mary Beth sat in a rocking chair, with her four-year-old napping on her lap. She raised a well-plucked eyebrow when she saw the state of Deborah's clothes, but she made no comment.

Deborah had hoped to catch Anna Maria alone, but it looked as if Mary Beth wasn't going to move for a while, so she said, "Do you know where I could find an attorney by the name of Bowers? He used to practice here."

"The Summer River Cemetery," Mary Beth said dryly. "Why? Are you two writing a prenuptial agreement or something?"

"Yes," Riley said promptly. "I'm trying to protect all my worldly goods from the possibility of Deb being a gold digger."

Deborah stared him into silence. "How about his partner, Milligan, or something like that? Is he still alive?"

"The last I knew, yes. What's wrong with having Rod draw it up?" Mary Beth countered.

"Conflict of interest," Riley said. "He might be prejudiced. For me, of course."

"Don't bet on it," his sister told him dryly. "He knows you too well. In any case, I'm not going to beg for your business. But I wouldn't count on Fred Milligan. He went to Springfield to join the attorney general's office, and is out of private practice."

Attorney general's office? Deborah thought blankly. There was a special division of the state attorney general's office that handled fraud; he would know immediately what she was talking about. That, plus the fact that Milligan also knew and understood the Lassiter trust. All she would have to do was catch up with Mr. Milligan!

She flung a triumphant look at Riley, who glared at her and suggested, a little too promptly, that it was time for them to be going if he was to be at the restaurant by the time the evening crowd began to appear. "I don't suppose you know where we'd find Alec?" he asked his sister.

"Don't worry about him," Mary Beth said. "I'll round him up when I take my brood home. One more scarcely makes a difference."

"Except to Robin, of course," Riley said under his breath as they left the house. "But if you think I'm going to argue with Mary Beth over custody of that little scoundrel..."

"Honestly, Riley, I expected you'd be applauding. The water balloon was a trick worthy of you at your worst."

"Do you really think so?" He grinned at her. "I must admit, I never thought of doing anything like that."

"I'm humbly grateful." But she promptly forgot the matter in her delight over her discovery, and she almost danced out to his car. "I told you Bowers and Milligan would be important," she said gleefully as soon as they were safely away from the farm.

Riley gave a sort of half-believing grunt. "We'll see how important it is. You can't do anything about it till Monday."

"Big deal. Oh." It was a very small voice.

Riley eyed her with almost malicious concern. "Yes, that still leaves us with the problem of Father Adams tomorrow."

"I don't want to lie to a man of the cloth, Riley."

"All you have to do is smile and stick to generalities."

"And you'll do the actual lying? You comfort me more than you can possibly know."

He gave her a sideways, speculative look. "For someone who doesn't want to go to church at all you have an awfully sensitive conscience," he mused. "I think we should tell him we want a spring wedding."

"All right," Deborah said agreeably. "We just won't tell him which spring."

"Something like that. Surely Ida won't start committing money right away when the wedding is months away."

"Obviously you haven't been involved in many weddings."

"And you have? Do tell, Debbie darling!"

"Remember all those girls who'll want to be bridesmaids at my wedding?" Deborah said dryly. "Half of them are already married, and I walked every one of them down the aisle. And held their hands through all the months of organizing and planning and budgeting...."

"Please, let's not talk about budgets," Riley said politely. "It makes my stomach ache."

"Mine, too," Deborah said glumly. "One of them took a full year, and it was on nothing like the scale Aunt Ida's got in mind. As a matter of fact, I can think of only one thing worse than having Aunt Ida planning my wedding, and that's watching her plan one for herself."

She was joking, and it startled her when Riley seemed to take her words seriously. He turned them over in his mind for almost a minute before he shook his head. "I don't think it will come to that," he said finally. "After all, the snake is getting everything he wants without any commitments, this way, and I don't see him changing that unless he has to."

It left her speechless.

They were almost back to Lassiter House before Riley said, "Correct me if I'm wrong, but I get the impression that you're not as sold on huge weddings as I thought you were."

Deborah was still thinking about the spectacle of an octogenarian bride in white satin and a veil—she would bet her life that Aunt Ida was eligible to wear one. On the other hand, she reminded herself, Aunt Ida was turning out to be full of surprises.

"Not exactly," she said absently. "My idea of a perfect wedding is a brief ceremony at nine in the morning, followed by a bash of a champagne brunch, followed by the departure of the bride and groom on a long, leisurely honeymoon in some romantic locale, not so far away that travel becomes a problem, and where there is nothing much to do but lie around and get to know each other."

Riley was grinning. "You could always pitch a tent at Paradise Lake," he said. "It sounds like just the place you're looking for!"

She made a face at him. "I said romantic, remember? But maybe I'll ask Preston to save me the bridal suite in his new hotel."

"That's an excellent idea if you're not planning to get married anytime in the next twenty years." He started to whistle, slightly off-key. She would have liked to hit him with something.

He drove all the way to the top of the hill, since he was only dropping her off; Deborah was grateful to avoid the climb, and when the car stopped under the porte cochere at the side of Lassiter House she said the most sincere thanks she had ever in her life expressed to Riley and got out.

"Hold it," he ordered, and came around the car.

"What? I said thank-you."

"Not nicely enough," he murmured. "At least, not if Ida's watching. And this house has a zillion windows, so she probably is."

The prospect of an audience never seemed to bother him, Deborah thought a little hazily, during one of the most thorough kisses she had ever participated in. It was almost funny, she decided, that without ever moving his hands out of safe and approved zones, Riley could make her feel as if she'd been sensually assaulted. Of course, there had been that brief, warm touch against her breast this afternoon, but that scarcely counted; it had only been a brush of his hand against her shirt, really, brought to a sudden end by the water balloon.

Still, it was just as well they'd been interrupted, she thought. She'd been enjoying the game perhaps a little too much for safety's sake. And as for the comment he had made last night that whoever had taught her to kiss should start a school, she thought, privately, that Riley could give a few lessons himself.

I wonder, she mused, *just where he learned all this....*

CHAPTER SEVEN

AUNT IDA HADN'T been watching. She was in the sun room at the back of the house, sitting on the wicker couch with a glossy magazine, so quiet and still that Deborah had almost stepped on the woman's toes before she realized she was there. Then, when she saw the photograph on the front cover of the magazine, she did her best to become invisible and sneak out before Ida noticed her. It was a vain effort, of course.

Aunt Ida waved the magazine in the air. "Look at this glorious white velvet gown," she said.

Deborah sighed inwardly. It was awfully warm in the sun room, with the afternoon light pouring through the beveled glass and not a breath of air moving, despite the open windows. How did Aunt Ida stand it? she wondered. Even more, how could the woman look admiringly at white velvet when the temperature inside Lassiter House must be above ninety degrees?

But talking about the temperature wouldn't make it cooler, so she obediently looked at the magazine. It was a beautiful dress, she had to admit, with a tailored bodice and a long full skirt sweeping to a short train. The collar was high and the beaded trim that twisted and curled across the soft velvet reminded her of military braid. The ensemble was something like a modified Cossack uniform, or was it only the fur headpiece that made her think of that? Yet somehow it was a very feminine dress, for an older and more sophisticated bride.

That's enough, Deborah, she told herself sternly. *Show the tiniest bit of interest and Aunt Ida will order it shipped by overnight mail!*

"I see leg-of-mutton sleeves are back in style again," she said with an air of casual unconcern.

"Yes. I swear, Deborah, I should have kept all those dresses I wore as a girl. They've been in and out of fashion a dozen times since then. I could have just had them remade."

Now that, Deborah thought, *sounds a great deal more like the Aunt Ida I remember!*

Ida held the magazine up at arm's length. "That headpiece is ermine," she remarked. "Lovely stuff. And velvet is always so elegant. Or would you rather have something in silk taffeta and marabou, or satin with an overlay of antique lace?" She glanced at Deborah's crumpled shorts and shirt, blinked and added dryly, "Though perhaps, to be on the safe side, you should consider something in polyester with a stain-resistant coating."

Deborah told herself that she should have seen that one coming. Razor-sharp sarcasm delivered without hesitation had always been Aunt Ida's strength, and there was no appropriate answer. "I'll think about it," she murmured.

Ida's gaze flickered as if she was disappointed by the meek response, but she said very smoothly, "When is the wedding going to be, anyway?"

"I don't know."

Aunt Ida cupped a hand behind her ear. "Do speak up, dear. It sounded as if you said you and Riley hadn't even discussed it."

Deborah gritted her teeth. "Riley said something about next spring." *There,* she thought. *That should be non-committal enough to slow her down.*

Aunt Ida almost clucked in concern. "Then we'll have to get busy. It will take every moment to be ready in time. What sort of theme are you going to have?"

Deborah was too startled to exercise caution. "A theme?" she asked weakly. "This isn't a high school prom, Aunt Ida."

"Of course not, but it should look as if it all goes together! Good heavens, Deborah, where is your head? I've always thought, for instance, that a summer wedding would be lovely with an ancient Grecian motif. Those high-waisted dresses in different pastel colors are so flattering, and there could be simple flowers in everyone's hair."

Deborah yielded to a sudden vision of Riley wearing a wreath of orange blossom, and had to turn a hysterical giggle into a choking cough. "I hadn't really considered a theme, Aunt Ida."

"Well, you should. Personally, I do love the Grecian idea. The wedding cake could be shaped like a miniature Parthenon...." She seemed to fade away for a minute, then went on briskly, as if she was resigned to the loss of her dream. "But I suppose spring would be a little cool for that style. And I doubt you'll want to wait a whole year from now if Riley wants to be married sooner."

Gladly, Deborah thought. *I'd wait any number of years!*

"Do think carefully about styles," Aunt Ida went on briskly. "I always think it's unfortunate when the brides-maids end up looking like dumplings in ruffles, don't you?"

"I'll keep it in mind," Deborah murmured. She didn't realize she was twisting the diamond ring on her finger. In fact, it was so light she'd forgotten she was wearing it, until Ida's pale blue eyes came to rest on it thoughtfully.

"That's not much of a ring," she remarked. "I'm surprised at Riley, giving you Darlene's diamond chip instead of a decent stone."

Deborah glanced down at her hand. Darlene? She had forgotten, if she had ever known, Riley's grandmother's name. Then, automatically, she sprang to the defense. "It's got great sentimental value," she said. "And I wouldn't want a big stone if Riley had to put himself in debt for it."

Ida gave a nasal grunt. "You could have a different ring, you know. The trust would pay for it."

And afterward I could pawn it to pay for the divorce, Deborah thought. For a split second it actually made sense. Then she wanted to bang her head against the nearest wall for letting herself get carried away.

Don't even think of things like that, she ordered herself. Riley's remark about going through with the ceremony was the craziest thing she had ever heard. In fact, all she had to do now was to talk to Milligan, and he would soon straighten Ida out. Voilà! There wouldn't be any bills, there certainly wouldn't be any wedding. And there wouldn't be any Paradise Valley, either.

She finally made her break to freedom, but only by taking along the stack of bride's magazines that Ida had already finished. The woman must have bought out the local newsstand rack, Deborah thought in disbelief as she tossed the pile on the end of the guest room bed. She flung herself down on the fainting couch by the window, fanning her hot face with one of the lighter magazines.

This, she thought, *is getting out of hand. I'm beginning to feel as if I'm never going to escape.*

Chicago, and the gallery, had never seemed so far away.

IDA WAS LATE coming down for dinner that night. Preston Powell wasn't, and his company quickly began to wear on Deborah's nerves. She didn't like being told that champagne was the only drink that could possibly match her own effervescence, or that her voice was like carillon bells in beauty and clarity. And when he announced, after an unnervingly close inspection, that her eyes were the very color of Paradise Lake on a stormy day, Deborah had had it.

She sipped her sherry and said, "I've been wondering about something, Preston. If someone makes an investment in your project, and then later changes his mind and wants a refund, what happens?"

She had to give him credit for poise; he didn't even hesitate. "I'd give it, of course," he said. "I don't want any unwilling investors. We're all a team, and one pessimistic person will affect us all." He sat down on the arm of her chair. "Has anyone ever told you—"

She moved away to stand by the baby grand piano, her fingers trailing over the keys. "You'd just give the money back?" Deborah mused.

"Well, not instantly, of course."

She was intrigued. How did the man enunciate without ever moving his lips? He didn't even stop smiling to talk!

"I'd want to know what had changed his mind," Preston went on, "and I'd do my best to convince him that he was turning his back on a perfect opportunity."

"But if he was sincere in wanting out?" she persisted.

"Then I'd write him a check for the full amount of his investment."

And our nameless, mythical investor had better be careful to get it to the bank right away, too, Deborah speculated.

Preston had followed her over to the piano. "Why all the questions, Deborah? Are you thinking of investing with me, and you want to be sure your money will be safe? I'd be happy to show you some projections."

The telephone bell shrilled stridently in the hall, and Deborah jumped. "I'd better get that," she said with a sigh of relief. "You know how Henry hates to be interrupted when he's putting the finishing touches on dinner."

It was Bristol, and for an instant when she heard that crisp, cultured Ivy League accent she was aghast, too upset even to speak. It wasn't only the idea of his calling her here at Lassiter House that was bothering her, she realized abruptly. It was the fact that she'd forgotten about him—in fact, she hadn't given him an instant's thought in the past two days. She hadn't missed him. She hadn't even wondered how he was, or how his business conference was progressing. Her mind had been so full of Riley.

My mind has been full of Paradise Valley, she corrected herself firmly. *Not of Riley. It's no surprise that I haven't been thinking of Bristol. I've had too many other things on my mind. And it's just as well, too, with the part I'm having to play.*

"Is there something wrong, my dear?" Bristol asked in the polite, careful tone she knew so well.

Deborah seized the last shreds of her poise. She could hardly tell him, after all, that he could not call her, unless she was willing to explain the whole plot. "Of course not. I was just surprised at hearing from you, that's all."

"But surely you know I would have called earlier if I hadn't been so very busy."

Heaven forbid, Deborah thought. "Are you enjoying San Francisco?"

There was a brief silence. "Darling, if I haven't had a spare moment to call you, surely you don't believe I've been out riding cable cars instead!"

"Of course not," Deborah said hastily. "How is the conference?"

"It's moving along wonderfully, thank you. There are so many implications for the foundation that it will take weeks to think them all through, of course. Ways to safely maximize the investment potential of the endowment funds, and—"

Deborah seized on one word. "Investment? Do you mean you're learning about all kinds of investments?"

There was another aching silence, and then Bristol said politely, "Yes, Deborah. I told you, I believe, that this was a seminar featuring the premier investment counselors of the nation. But perhaps you were preoccupied at the time."

They'd been at Coq au Vin, and she'd been thinking of Riley; she remembered it, now. "I don't suppose they'd know anything about a resort development here in Summerset."

He laughed condescendingly. "My dear, these people keep track of everything. I'm sure they'd know. Are you looking for some free advice, or merely offering me a test case to use to evaluate their knowledge?"

"Neither. I'd just like to find out everything I can. Aunt Ida's got herself into this scheme, you see, and—"

"Oh, yes, your Aunt Ida. How is the dear old lady?"

For one mad moment, Deborah considered telling him about Aunt Ida, the wedding czar of Summerset. Then she regained control of herself. She shot a look over her shoulder toward the parlor where Preston Powell was still drinking his Manhattan, and said in a low voice, "Look, Bristol, I can't take the time to give you all the details, but this is important. If you can find out anything for me about Paradise Valley, and Preston Powell, the guy who's promoting it . . .''

To Bristol's credit, he didn't demand an explanation. He had her spell Preston's name and that of the resort, and he said, "She's financially over her head, do you think? It's such a shame, but these things do happen now and then. I'll see what I can do to help rescue the dear lady and put your mind at rest, Deborah."

After he'd said goodbye she sat there for a long moment with the telephone still in her hand. *Good old Bristol,* she thought. Always solid and predictable, and *there.* He was everything that Morgan had never been. What was it Riley had called Morgan? Her furry-faced friend? She smiled a little at the implication. He *had* been something of an animal, interested mainly in his own comfort.

Ida came down the staircase, her old-fashioned square-heeled shoes striking solidly against the wooden steps. "I do hope you're not going to expect us to delay dinner while you chat," she said.

"Of course not," Deborah said cordially. *In fact,* she thought, *I can't wait for dinner to be over, so I can get out of this madhouse and go bring Riley up-to-date. I had no idea that conspiracy was a full-time job!*

IT HAD APPARENTLY BEEN a slow night at the restaurant. Cars were sparse around the warehouse, and while she was parking she saw a figure in dark clothing silhouetted against the gathering twilight, leaning against the railing that separated the parking area from the drop to the river itself.

Riley turned from the rail and watched her come toward him. "That's a switch," he said, with a wave of his hand at her cocktail dress, a drifty thing in emerald green shot through with gold threads.

"I was trying to impress Aunt Ida," she said. "What are you doing out here?"

Riley grinned. "Don't you know?" He pointed down at the water. "I'm reflecting."

Deborah groaned. "I'm amazed that your mother didn't drown you by the time you were six."

"I resent that. I was a darling six-year-old. You, on the other hand, were a pudgy crybaby. Of course, that was nothing compared to what you were like at nine, when you started to giggle and didn't stop for two years. And then when you were twelve, you had braces as well as baby fat."

"Don't you ever forget anything? It's very troublesome of you, Riley." It should have annoyed her, she thought, having every embarrassing incident of her childhood dangled over her head that way. But somehow, it didn't bother her anymore. In a way, she thought, it was rather pleasant to spend time with someone who knew every fracture, every fault, every wrinkle in her past. It was comfortable not to have to hide anything.

Not that she hid things from Bristol, exactly, she thought uncomfortably. It was just that there were subjects that never came up; childhood memories, and silly, unimportant, almost forgotten things like that. With Riley it was different. He might know every embarrassing detail there was to know about her, but she knew every wart on his character, too. They were even.

He leaned against the rail and looked at her for a long time. "You know what, kid?" he said finally. "You turned out pretty decent despite it all."

She pretended irritation. "Oh, is that all you can say for me? I'm pretty decent?"

He grinned. "What do you want? A poem? All right. 'Roses are red, and Debbie is blue, because I won't tell her she's beautiful, too.'"

She reached up to tousle his hair. He caught her wrists and twisted her around—how, she was not quite sure—until she was firmly held between his body and the railing, with her back to him, his arms around her, her hands under his on the cool steel bar. She wriggled a little and then gave up with dignity. He hadn't been on the high school wrestling team for nothing.

The last rays of sunshine had turned the smooth surface of the river to liquid gold, tinged with violet and pink and blue.

Beautiful, Deborah was thinking idly. *Did he mean that he does think I'm beautiful, and just won't feed my vanity by telling me, or did he mean that he has too much integrity to say something that isn't true? I wonder which it is.*

She tipped back her head to look thoughtfully up at him. Sunset's glow had caught in his hair, turning the auburn threads to strands of fire. Deborah's breath caught in her throat.

He really has turned out to be one very good-looking man, she thought. But it wasn't only looks that made him attractive. There were lots of handsome men, but Riley was one of the rare ones who weren't stuck on themselves. The combination was deadly.

Good heavens, Deborah thought, *he might have been telling the simple truth when he said there were hundreds of women in his life! If someone had asked me two weeks ago about my cousin Riley, the great lover, I'd have laughed till I choked. But at the moment it doesn't sound very funny. Even I . . .*

Even I . . . what?

She swallowed hard and told herself deliberately, *Even I have enjoyed his kisses. So what's wrong with that? Why*

*shouldn't I have a little fun? I'm no prude, and I'm not a
hypocrite, either.*

They watched in silence until the fiery glow in the west
had died to shades of velvety gray, and streetlights began
to form a glittering chain along the avenue that bordered
the river.

Riley cleared his throat. "Seeing that always makes me
want to go get my trumpet and play 'Taps.'"

"I thought 'Taps' called for a bugle," Deborah mused.
Her voice was husky, and she had to clear her throat.

"Sorry. I can't play a bugle."

She smiled up at him warmly. "Of course, you could
never play the trumpet worth a darn, either." His arms
tightened threateningly, and she said very quickly, "I
didn't mean that, of course. Have you had a chance to talk
to Ruth?"

Riley let her go. "Not yet," he said slowly. "And what
in heaven's name am I supposed to tell her, anyway?"

It was chilly with the sun gone. Deborah turned her back
to the rail and told him of Preston's offer to refund money
to any unhappy investor.

Riley grunted. "I wouldn't care to make any bets on
that. I doubt he's put it in writing anywhere. But I'll tell
her."

"You don't think she'll change her mind?"

"No. And she may tell me to go to hell, that it's none of
my business what she does with her money. And it's not,
you know, but I suppose I have to try."

"For Alec's sake," Deborah reminded gently. When he
didn't answer, she nudged him. "Riley?"

"I'm thinking about it," he said. "After that water
balloon this afternoon, I'm not so sure."

"That's always the way with practical jokers," Deborah said. "They're poor sports themselves. Oh, I have

good news, by the way. Father Adams is busy with a christening brunch after services tomorrow and can't talk to us until Wednesday.''

"That's a relief."

"It certainly is. With any luck at all we'll be history by Wednesday, and there won't be any need to draw him into it at all."

"You think it will be that fast?" Riley said doubtfully.

"Of course. I'll call Milligan on Monday and explain what's going on, he'll call Aunt Ida and read her the riot act, and we'll be in the clear."

"By Wednesday." He sounded dissatisfied.

"Why not?" Deborah asked grandly. "I've left him Tuesday to ask around about Preston Powell. That should be plenty of time."

"You never cease to amaze me, Debbie darling." There was faint irony in his voice.

Deborah, who had been about to tell him that Bristol was now also on the trail, changed her mind. So Riley didn't think she could accomplish anything, hmm? Well, just let him wait; sooner or later he'd see what she could do!

"I'm not trying to break up the party," Riley said, "but I did just step out for a breath of fresh air, and by now the staff must be ready to report me as missing. Would you like to come in and have dessert while I close up the place?"

"Are you trying to corrupt me?"

His eyes brightened. "That depends. Are you corruptible?"

"I was referring to that cartload of calories I saw Ruth wheeling around last night," Deborah said with dignity.

"Well, you're certainly no fun at all. As a matter of fact, however, I happen to know that the dessert menu at Lassiter House consists of fruit with gelatin, or for a change now and then, gelatin with fruit.''

Deborah sighed. ''You're right, and it's not fresh fruit at that.''

The dessert cart was just as tempting as she remembered it, and she fought a brief skirmish with her conscience before surrendering to the lure of a raspberry puff pastry, oozing whipped cream and nestled in a pool of caramel sauce on a crystal plate. She perched on a high stool at the bar to eat it, and was only halfway through when Riley appeared. He raised an eyebrow, but he didn't comment. He didn't have to; she knew what he was thinking.

Deborah speared a raspberry on the tines of her fork and waved it at him. ''Fresh fruit,'' she said. ''From your mother's garden, I presume?''

He caught her wrist and held it while he ate the berry. ''Of course. The doors are locked, and everybody's gone.''

''I know. I said good-night to Ruth. Did you talk to her?''

''With everyone around? Of course not. And I didn't exactly want to ask her to stay late.''

Deborah nodded wisely. ''The hostess wouldn't have liked that at all,'' she murmured, and licked her fork. ''I take back what I said about Ruth being infatuated with you,'' she went on. ''It's the hostess I think you should watch out for. What is her name, anyway?''

''Suzannah. She prefers being called Zanne.''

Deborah nodded. ''It would be something like that. She doesn't like me, you know.''

''She can't possibly have formed an opinion.''

''Of course she can. I've got the prize. You.'' She frowned and dipped her fork into the caramel again, then let the sauce trail in strands over the top of the pastry.

"If you've finished playing with that—"

"I'm not playing with it. And I'm not finished."

"Then bring it along, but let's go somewhere that's more comfortable than this, all right?" He turned out the lights. Deborah obediently picked up her plate and followed him through the dim glow of the security lights through the lobby and up the stairs.

"What's up here?" she asked, peering into the darkness at the first landing. "You've got the restaurant on the ground floor and your apartment at the top, but what's in between?"

"Lots of empty space," Riley said. "Would you like the tour?"

Deborah shook her head. "Not really. It was merely curiosity."

But he had already pulled out a ring of keys and unlocked a door. Bare fluorescent fixtures hummed quietly into life, casting a bluish glow over the single empty room that took up the entire floor. It was scrupulously clean, but the walls were bare brick, and the scratches and stains on the wooden floor were mute evidence of hard use. No amount of scrubbing could wipe them out. The ceiling had once been lined with acoustic tiles, but a good many of them were gone, and in the gaps Deborah could see the original ceiling level. The room was almost tall enough for a balcony to be added, she thought. It would make wonderful studio apartments.

She must have said something aloud, but she didn't realize it, and it startled her when Riley spoke. "I'd rather turn it into extra party rooms for the restaurant," he said. "As it is, when I've got a big dinner party or reception, I have to turn my regular customers away. But that's a long while off."

"Why? You've got the space, and you certainly need it."

"Remember what you said about the appearance of success not being cheap? Besides, have you priced elevators lately, Debbie darling?" He turned off the lights and snapped the lock tight. "There are regulations about things like that. And that's only the beginning. I also own the building next door."

She looked at him in astonishment.

"You may well ask why," Riley murmured. "I was having a weak moment, and the price was really ridiculously low, that's why. I'd like to turn it into a collection of antique shops or something of the sort."

"It would draw customers into the neighborhood," she said.

"Bright girl. And after doing all that shopping, they'd be hungry, too. But by the time I got the leaks fixed in the roof, and all the broken glass repaired . . ." He sighed. "Maybe next year, if the snake doesn't succeed in throwing the whole town into an economic slump in the meantime."

They were at the door of his apartment. "He could do that?"

"Certainly. If he siphons off enough of the disposable cash that would otherwise have supported Summerset businesses."

"I see." Deborah had lost her appetite, and her voice sounded hollow.

"But of course there's no reason for concern, is there?" Riley's tone was light. "You're going to have it all fixed up by Wednesday."

The weight of what she was trying to do, of the responsibility she had taken on, was suddenly overwhelming. Deborah set down the crystal plate with a little crash and put one hand to her temple, where a blood vessel was throbbing with an alarming rhythm.

He turned from closing the door and said, "Deb? Are you all right?" He was beside her in two steps, his arms closing gently around her, taking her weight against him as her knees gave way. He carried her to the overstuffed couch and dropped to one knee beside her, his hand warm against her cheek. "Debbie darling, what is it?"

She tried to tell him, incoherent as she was, and he frowned through her sobs and tears and half sentences. Halfway through her attempt to explain, he moved to the couch and put both arms around her. Finally he seemed to have it all put together. "Is that all?" he said.

"All!" She was irate. "You're the one who said—"

"Dammit, Debbie, I was only teasing you. Don't take it so seriously."

"That was teasing?" She sat up straight and pushed him away.

"All right, it wasn't very tactful, but you were beginning to sound all-powerful, you know. It's not up to you to save the world."

"Only your corner of it, is that all?"

"Just try, Debbie. If it doesn't work—"

"Then your dreams go down the drain." Despite herself, she knew she sounded a little sad about that, and when his arm tightened, pulling her back against him, she didn't object.

Riley rubbed his chin against her hair. "Not me," he said gently. "Don't worry about me. And as for everyone else, well, it's a sad fact, but true, that everybody's got a right to be a damn fool, Deb."

He stopped. She sniffed, and nodded, and looked up at him, waiting for him to continue, and something in his face seemed to hold her paralyzed.

Riley sighed. "Including me," he said under his breath. The palm of his hand flattened against the middle of her back and pulled her close against him.

She didn't resist. In fact, if she had been able to express what she was thinking in that moment, she would probably have said that she didn't in the least mind the idea of a soft, comforting caress.

But that was far from the reality. There was no softness, no caressing comfort, in the way he kissed her. It was instead more like a summer thunderstorm that sprang fully developed from a clear sky, raging with thunder and lightning and wind, threatening anything that lay in its way, anything foolish enough not to seek shelter.

But she did not want to run for shelter. She did not want to hide herself from the storm. And so she kissed him in return and gloried in the taste of him, in the firmness of his body against hers as he eased her back against the overstuffed couch, and in the gentle touch of his hands against the thin emerald green of her dress. It was a sensation not much different than if he had actually been touching the heat-flushed skin underneath. And in a moment, she knew, he would be, for his fingers had gone unerringly to the tiny buttons that fastened the front of the dress.

You should stop this, she told herself. *This is like playing Russian roulette. The longer it goes on the more dangerous it gets. You must stop this, Deborah....*

But what actually came out of her mouth, in a feeble sort of croak, was, "Not here, Riley."

He did not unfasten the dress. Instead his hands slid down over the soft fabric until his palms were resting firmly over her breasts. The soft tips contracted under his touch, and an uncontrollable shiver racked her body.

It was not fear, she diagnosed with the one bit of her brain that still seemed to be functioning correctly. Certainly she was not afraid of Riley.

But was he afraid of her? He looked a little pale, Deborah thought, as he pushed himself up and away from her, and rubbed his hand along his jaw.

She tried to laugh. "We just proved we're capable," she said unsteadily, and then realized that there were a dozen ways to interpret that. "Of being damn fools, I mean."

"Yes," Riley muttered. "Well. If there isn't any further business tonight, I mean, anything more to talk about..."

Deborah gathered herself together and surreptitiously tried out her feet to make sure they still worked before she attempted to stand up. "Nothing," she said. "I'll see you sometime tomorrow then."

"I'll take you home."

"I've got my car, Riley."

"So I'll ride up with you and walk back."

"Honestly, I'll be fine! I drive around Chicago at night, you know."

"You'll be perfectly safe from me, too," he said levelly. "But you don't want Ida asking questions about why you came home alone, do you?"

That silenced her, and they walked down the long flights of stairs and out to the Jaguar without another word. Unlike the previous night, he made no effort to take her keys, and when she had parked the car at Lassiter House he gave her the merest brush of his lips against her cheek, and then, rather than walking her all the way up to the house, leaned against the car and watched until she was safely at the front door.

She glanced back at him from the terrace. He was a mere dark shadow in the little parking area halfway down the hill. As she watched, he seemed to merge with the night, and vanish.

That puts you in your place, Deborah told herself. *You scared the poor man to death, that's obvious.* Not here, Riley. *Good heavens, girl, you sounded like an overheated nymphomaniac. Fortunate for you that he didn't have the opposite reaction! Just what would you have done if he'd taken you at your word and led you off to his bedroom?*

You'd have gone, said the tiny voice of conscience. *And you'd have loved it.*

CHAPTER EIGHT

AND THAT, she told herself sternly, *would have been the most deranged thing you could possibly have done.* Going to bed with Riley was utterly out of the question. Certainly he was attractive. She could understand why women found him appealing, even why some of them fell in love with him. But Deborah Ainsley was not among them.

Or am I? she asked herself, half-astonished by the force of the question.

Love? It was insane, and yet...

She sat down on the bench of the carved walnut coat tree in the hall, and didn't even notice that the plush padding, the best available in Jacob's day, was no longer adequate.

I can't have fallen in love with Riley, she told herself desperately. *Yes, it's true that he grew up to be a decent human being, despite all indications to the contrary when he was younger, but that's certainly no reason for me to fall in love with him. It's just that I'm stuck here in Summerset, with only Riley to confide in. When I get back to Chicago, back to Bristol, I'll laugh at the notion that I could have fallen for Riley.*

Bristol. She seized on his name with a lighter heart, and was in her room before she remembered the odd feeling she'd had when he called earlier that evening, as if he was phoning from another planet altogether. How had she managed to tuck Bristol so far away into a corner of her heart that she hadn't even thought of him in two days? The resort, she told herself. Aunt Ida, Preston Powell, Ruth, the trust. It was no wonder she hadn't had time to day-dream about Bristol.

She perched on the marble ledge of the open window and looked down across the town, where the stillness of night lay almost undisturbed under the moon's glow. In the quietness, the truth could not be denied.

It was not the resort and Aunt Ida and the trust that had kept her from thinking about Bristol, she admitted with slow and painful honesty. It was Riley who had inter-fered. The evidence was clear. Tonight, when she was with Riley, she had yet again forgotten Bristol altogether.

It's not important, she told herself firmly. *It's not as if you were being unfaithful to Bristol, after all. You've made no promises to him. It would be a different matter alto-gether if you were engaged to him, if you were wearing his ring.*

She looked for a long time at Darlene Lassiter's dia-mond, sparkling faintly on her finger. Then, with confu-sion in her heart, she undressed in the dark and crept into her bed. Surely, in the morning, everything would once more make sense.

ON SUNDAY MORNING, Deborah discovered that Preston Powell did not, after all, spend every minute of his time on the golf course. Despite the lure of a perfect, sunny day, he came downstairs dressed in somber black and joined her and Aunt Ida in the back of the vintage Rolls for the short trip down the hill to the old stone church.

Deborah's heart skittered from toes to throat for most of the trip; she wasn't certain if it was because of Pres-ton's presence or Henry's driving skills, which were rusty at best. Or, perhaps, it was her fear that Aunt Ida might prevail upon Father Adams to fit them into his morning's schedule after all. Or . . .

She maneuvered into the pew first, to keep Aunt Ida between her and Preston, and spent the few minutes before the service began in refreshing her memories of the church. It really was not as huge and imposing as she had thought when she was a child and the stained glass wasn't garish at all. It was brilliantly jeweled and gloriously rich, a superb Victorian legacy.

The organ prelude had already begun when Riley came quickly down the side aisle and slid into the pew beside her. Late, she thought crisply, and remembered what Mary Beth had said about his habits. Then she realized what had really been bothering her earlier. It had not been Preston Powell or Henry, or even the prospect of a chat with Father Adams, but the fear that Riley wouldn't show up at all, that what had happened between them last night had shaken him so badly that nothing else mattered anymore.

He smiled at her, a smile that didn't quite reach his eyes, and picked up the hymnbook from the rack just as Father Adams began the service. The rich baritone rolled down over the congregation, and Deborah closed her eyes and imagined the way it would sound if the words were just a little different, if he was starting out instead with ''Dearly beloved, we are gathered here today to witness the union of this man and this woman in holy matrimony. . . .''

Her heart twisted a little, and it was then that she finally faced the truth. Last night it had not been imagination that had led to her suspicions that she had fallen in love with Riley. It had not been hormones running wild, or boredom with the lack of company in Summerset, that had sent her into his arms. The simple truth was that it wouldn't have mattered where she was; as long as Riley was there, too, she would have been content. The peacefulness she felt when she was with him—the comfortable feeling of having nothing to hide—those had been the symptoms of growing love, and she had been too innocent, or too egotistical, to recognize them. She had gone merrily on her way, falling harder with every moment she spent in his company.

Everybody's got a right to be a damn fool, Riley had said last night. *It's true,* she thought. *And I've certainly exercised my right to be a fool by falling in love with him.*

She kept her head bent respectfully, but she didn't hear much of the service. Her imagination kept filling in bits from the dozens of weddings she had attended. But it wasn't the elaborate decorations or the glorious voice of a professional musician or the glamorous costumes that she recalled. It was the beauty of the ritual, and the love that spilled across the church, and the softness in a young man's eyes as his bride came to him....

The dresses, the flowers, the music, the party, they were nice, to help set the stage, but all those things meant nothing at all, really. What mattered was the person who shared the hopes and the dreams, and the love that was more important than any material things.

She looked down at her left hand, at Darlene Lassiter's diamond ring. It was such a tiny thing, but it had meant so much to Riley's grandmother. It had been the symbol of her love, and the gift of the man who loved her. That had been enough. The number of carats mattered nothing, compared to that.

It would have been enough for me, too, Deborah thought humbly. *If only Riley had loved me. If only that easy companionship we felt had grown into something more for him, as it did for me.*

But it had not. And now even the easy companionship they had shared was a thing of the past. For now Deborah would have to keep up her guard, even if Riley offered her a return to the way things had been.

She could not bear it if he knew, and felt sorry for her, or even worse, if he was amused. She could not allow him to guess what had happened to her. And so she must guard herself with care, for now she had something that she must, at all costs, hide from the man she loved.

DEBORAH INTENDED to start her search for Fred Milligan at the earliest moment that the attorney general's office could possibly be open on Monday morning. The guest room's solar alarm clock did not fail her, though she moaned in resignation as usual when the sunlight crept across her pillow and into her eyes.

What she did not expect was to run into Aunt Ida at the breakfast table. *It's not fair,* she thought, as Ida looked at her with a mixture of approval and skepticism, or was that just Deborah's own guilty conscience speaking? She slid warily into her chair with a surreptitious glance at her wristwatch. No, it wasn't her imagination; it might be early for her, but it was certainly late for Aunt Ida to be still lingering over her coffee.

"It's nice to see you taking advantage of the best part of the day," Aunt Ida said calmly. "I'm glad you're up, Deborah. I need you to do a small favor for me this morning."

Deborah sighed inwardly as she poured herself a glass of orange juice. *Great,* she thought. *Just what I need. She's probably decided to teach me to prune the roses, on the very day when I absolutely must get out of here and to a telephone where I can't be overheard. Now what do I do?* she wondered. *What kind of excuse can I safely give?*

"I was planning to go down to the restaurant," she said tentatively.

Ida dismissed that with a wave of her hand. "It won't even be open for hours, and I'm sure you won't mind delaying your plans briefly. Henry will be out doing the marketing, you see, and Preston—"

"I know," Deborah said glumly. "He's on the golf course making up for yesterday."

Ida looked at her sharply. "As it happens, he's out at Paradise Valley, but that's beside the point. Someone has to be here this morning to let in the real estate agent."

Deborah choked on her orange juice. "The— Do you mean someone's coming to look at Lassiter House? Today?"

"Is there a reason why they shouldn't?" Ida asked crisply. "I'd take care of the matter myself, but I've been advised it's wiser for the owner to be absent when the house is shown."

I can't quarrel with that, Deborah thought. *Especially in this case.*

"All you have to do, really, is let them in. It isn't as if you'd be giving a tour or anything of the sort, and it won't take long. I just want to have someone here." Aunt Ida wiped her lips primly with her linen napkin and pushed back her chair. "I do so appreciate your help, Deborah."

And that, Deborah told herself wryly, *is that!*

Though, when she thought about it, it wouldn't be so terrible after all. With Ida gone, there was no reason she couldn't go right ahead with her call from Lassiter House. And there was poetic justice, as well as a bit of black humor, in the idea of telephoning Fred Milligan from Aunt Ida's own house, and charging the call to her bill.

Ida stopped at the door. "I've been meaning to ask you, Deborah," she went on. "This gallery of yours, in Chicago?"

Deborah braced herself.

"You're going to give it up, of course."

It was not a question, and it set Deborah's hair on end, despite Riley's warnings that the matter was certain to arise. "Why should I?" she asked coolly. "I might just take on a partner to run the Chicago operation, and start a branch office here."

Ida's eyebrows raised. "What a lovely idea," she said. "In Riley's extra building, no doubt? I'm glad you've given it so much thought. It's a much more prudent plan than for you to actually work for him as a hostess, or anything of that sort, until the children come along." She smiled approvingly and vanished toward the kitchen, calling Henry's name.

Deborah finished her orange juice slowly and deliberately, and waited for Ida to leave the house. She was getting an awful lot of experience in practicing patience, she thought. It would no doubt come in handy sometime.

But there was a pang of sadness in knowing that whatever happened, it would soon be finished. She would be back in Chicago, and these few days in Summerset would be history. In time, they would fade into distant memory.

And pigs will fly, too, she told herself tartly. It wasn't going to be so easy to forget the day at the farm, and the long warm evenings at Riley's apartment. Even yesterday at church and through a long afternoon at Lassiter House, despite that new undercurrent of uneasiness between them, there had been moments of warm harmony, of shared laughter, of joy.

Because, Deborah told herself honestly, *in those moments I forgot that it was only a scene we were playing, and I allowed myself to believe that the way he held my hand and looked at me was the reality.*

It was something of a miracle that she actually reached Fred Milligan on her second try, though it was only by talking very fast and using Ida's name to his secretary. Fred Milligan himself listened to her in such utter silence that Deborah began to wonder if he was still there at all, or if he had put down the telephone and gone off.

She broke off in midsentence. "Mr. Milligan?" she asked anxiously.

He grunted. "I'm still here, Miss Ainsley. So far you've told me that you think Ida's lost any business sense she ever had, but frankly I don't see why you're trying to get me involved in it."

"But surely you have some influence with her still!"

"Perhaps I do, and perhaps not. It's her own business, you know."

"Not entirely," Deborah said pointedly.

"Oh, yes. Now we're getting to the bottom of it. It's your trust fund you're really concerned about, isn't it?"

"It isn't exactly criminal to want to see it preserved, is it?" she snapped, and then thought better of it. "I'm not a gold digger, Mr. Milligan. I'm worried about Aunt Ida, and how she'll take it if—when—Preston Powell disappears with her cash and leaves her holding the bag. She's not a young woman, and the shock—"

The doorbell rang. Deborah looked distractedly toward the front of the house and then told herself that it would just have to wait. She propped her elbow on the small telephone table and put her head down into her palm.

"The preservation of the capital is certainly a concern," she went on steadily. "But it's not the only thing that is important to me. I do not want to see Aunt Ida defrauded and hurt."

Fred Milligan grunted again. "Very well, I'll talk to her as soon as I can," he said finally, with obvious resignation.

"Mr. Milligan, you have my deepest gratitude—"

"Don't thank me," he said bluntly. "I haven't done anything yet, and I'm not sure I will. Anything more than to talk to her, that is."

"That's all I've asked for," Deborah said pointedly. She would have hung up on him if he had given her a chance.

The doorbell pealed again, longer and seemingly louder this time. She swore under her breath and hurried down the long hall to answer it.

The real estate agent still had his finger on the bell when Deborah opened the door. The prospective buyers, a couple in their late thirties, were standing on the terrace, inspecting the roof through binoculars. They were no sooner inside the house than the woman wrinkled her nose and made a comment about the musty smell. Deborah had thought the same thing herself a hundred times, but she found herself resenting the remark from a stranger and wanting to usher the woman straight back out into the sunshine. Instead, she smiled cheerfully and retreated to her perch in the telephone booth in the back hallway while the real estate agent and the prospective buyers began their tour.

The telephone at the gallery rang several times, and Peggy sounded a bit out of breath when she answered it.

"I'll call back if you're busy," Deborah offered.

"Oh, no—no clients, that is. I was unpacking crates of sculpture that just came in from Michigan."

"How does it all look?"

"Wonderful, I think. It's just that there's so much of it, and I've got no room to put it! Deborah, have you considered renting the building next door and expanding?"

"Frequently." It was crisp. "But you know what rents are like on the Magnificent Mile."

"I know," Peggy said with resignation. "Well, I'll fit it all in somehow. When are you going to be back?"

Deborah forced herself to laugh. "Don't worry. You've got a couple of days to work it out." She broke the connection and sat with the telephone in her hand, thinking glumly that if Ida persisted with her scheme, the Ainsley Gallery not only wouldn't be expanding, but she would probably be looking for a new and less expensive location altogether. It was not a pleasant thought, and to help banish it, she called her father at the foundation offices.

He was, as usual, cheerful. "Hello, darling. Is there something you want me to bring down for you?"

"You're coming to Summerset? Daddy, are you sure that's wise?"

"Didn't Ida tell you? She called me up yesterday and said she thought I should be there for your chat with the Reverend whatever-his-name-is, and of course I agreed." He chuckled. "It sounds as if you and Riley are doing a capital job with her!"

Deborah groaned. "Oh, we are. You should have been here yesterday, when she told us she didn't think the church would be big enough to hold everyone on her guest list and perhaps we should have the wedding in the high school auditorium where they held Uncle Ralph's funeral. Daddy, I can't take much more of this. You've got some influence at the state level, don't you?"

"Well, a bit perhaps. But—"

She told him about Fred Milligan. "And if you could just hint that your friend the governor might fire him if he doesn't cooperate . . ." she suggested.

"You're certainly sounding bloodthirsty. I'll see what I can do, and I'll be there tomorrow, darling, so go cry on Riley's shoulder if you need to, but don't say a word to Ida in the meantime. Everything will be all right. It's only a temporary measure, after all, and you'll be out of this mess before you know it."

Cry on Riley's shoulder? Deborah thought despairingly. *About what, for heaven's sake?* The only thing that made her feel like crying was the fact that she didn't really want to be out of this mess. If only she could rearrange it a bit, this engagement would be not a nightmare, but a dream come true.

And if she told Riley that, he would be the one doing the crying, she told herself grimly. Unless that irrepressible sense of humor took over and he started to laugh instead.

She had almost forgotten the prospective buyers, until the clatter of feet descending the stairs reminded her. They stopped at the bottom, and in the quiet house Deborah could hear every word as the woman said, "It's not perfect, of course, but it's certainly got atmosphere, and we can make it work. In a way it's an advantage that it hasn't been remodeled or updated at all."

Deborah wanted to scream. She hoped Fred Milligan managed to make time to call Aunt Ida today. Tomorrow might be too late.

WITH HER TELEPHONE CALLS completed, there was no reason for her to go to the restaurant, but she found herself there anyway. Riley would want to know what had happened, she told herself, and squashed the tiny voice in the back of her brain that said she really had nothing to report and so it was only her desire to see him again that had brought her hotfooting it down to the old warehouse.

The back door was unlocked, but there was no answer at all when she called his name, so she went on in. She peeked into a pantry lined with boxes and crates and tubs, walked through the gleaming stainless steel kitchen where huge coolers hummed as if to keep themselves company, and almost tiptoed through the ghostly-silent dining room.

Riley was in his office, and the surface of his desk was buried in bills and invoices and order forms and payroll records. His hair was rumpled; it was obvious he'd been running his fingers through it.

He didn't even bother to say hello. "You can use the phone in the bar. There won't be anyone around, and I've got to get through my bookkeeping this morning."

Deborah gingerly pushed papers back from the corner of his desk and perched on it. "I can see this is one of your favorite pastimes," she said, and waved a hand at the papers. "You look so very cheerful about it."

He gave a little snort. "Taking a few days off almost isn't worth it," he muttered, "with all the catching up there is to do."

"How well I know," she said, thinking of her own desk at the gallery. It was not an inviting prospect. "I don't need the phone, by the way. I've already reached Mr. Milligan."

He looked up at her warily. "And?"

"And he's going to talk to Aunt Ida."

He looked astounded, and then slowly warmth dawned in his eyes. "Good girl!"

Being on the receiving end of Riley's smile, she thought, was almost better than getting a trophy, and it was a long moment before she remembered that she wasn't as certain of her overall success as he seemed to be. But before she could warn him that Fred Milligan hadn't exactly promised to help them out, Riley had picked up his pen again.

"Mary Beth and Rod are having a party here tonight," he said, reaching for another envelope. "She wants us to join them."

"Great," Deborah muttered. "That's all I need, more people asking stupid questions."

"I don't suppose we have to go, but she was rather insistent."

"I'll bet she was." When Mary Beth wanted something, she could give new meaning to the word *insistent*.

Deborah saw what looked like her father's handwriting on the face of a fat envelope half-hidden under Riley's elbow, and she tried to twist her head to an impossible angle so she could inspect it more closely.

"She said she tried to call you at Lassiter House, but she couldn't get through."

"I don't doubt it." It sounded absentminded; she was still studying the penmanship. It was definitely William's, she decided.

Riley shifted his elbow and the envelope fell off the desk. "What's eating you this morning? Oh, people asking stupid questions. Has Ida started in on you again?"

"Whatever makes you think she might?" Deborah's voice was only faintly ironic; she was proud of herself. "She's been relatively calm since that outburst yesterday, and frankly, the lull terrifies me. Oh, this morning she approved my plans to open a branch gallery in your extra building, but other than that—"

Riley pushed back his chair and propped his feet on the corner of his desk. "That's not a bad idea at all," he said thoughtfully. "A high-class gallery, perhaps not quite as upscale as your Chicago operation, but with the same sort of style."

It did sound wonderful. In fact, Deborah could see it, without even having to close her eyes and imagine; a reincarnated Ainsley Gallery seemed to have sprung to life in her head in the space of an instant. She could have an entire floor—who cared if it had once been a warehouse? All the evidence of that could be erased easily enough. There would be high ceilings and natural light and airy space. The kind of space that she could never afford in Chicago.

Not possible, she reminded herself. *Because whether you stay on Michigan Avenue or not, you'll be in Chicago. Not here in Summerset.*

She shook her head. "Remodeling would take a ton of money," she said. The repressive tone of voice should have ended the conversation, but she'd forgotten for a moment that she wasn't talking to the average man, but to Riley.

"That's no problem. Not if Ida approves."

"What on earth do you mean?"

He sat up and began scrambling through the papers on his desk. "It's here somewhere... I was reading it just a little while ago."

"If you're talking about the copy of the trust document that Daddy sent," she said coolly, "I believe you'll find it under the wheels of your chair. And what do you mean, you were reading it?"

He grinned at her. "Well, it was addressed to me," he pointed out reasonably. "In fact, it's marked *Personal.*" He stooped to retrieve the envelope and waved it at her with a flourish. "The trust allows you to get cash to develop a business opportunity, with the trustees' approval."

Deborah seized the envelope out of his hand. "No one ever told me that before!"

He shrugged. "Perhaps Ida didn't approve of your location in Chicago."

She buried her nose in the document, several closely spaced pages of legalese that soon had her floundering. "I can't believe this," she said. "No wonder Daddy always let the attorneys handle it. Listen to this bit."

Riley stopped writing a check and looked up at her. "I've read that bit," he pointed out. "And all the other bits, too. Would you mind doing that somewhere else? You make a very attractive paperweight, but I do need to get down to work.''

"I'm so sorry," she said sweetly, and slid off the desk. "I thought perhaps you'd agree that this was important."

He didn't even answer, and she stalked back through the restaurant and out to her car in a huff.

"Don't be ridiculous," she told herself. "The man does have a job, after all, and he's running behind because he must have spent an hour or two this morning deciphering this mess." She tossed the envelope onto the dashboard. "What are you fussing about, anyway? The fact that you didn't even get a kiss?"

It stopped her cold, because it was true.

Remember that, she told herself firmly. *Remember it well.* Today, he had not had an audience that needed to be impressed, and apparently he'd done all the research he felt necessary. So he had stopped exerting his right to be a damned fool....

She waved at Alec, who was walking his bicycle along Main Street, and was a block past him before she realized that the front tire on the bike had been flat. She circled the block, pulled up beside him and called, "Need a lift somewhere?"

They managed to wedge the bicycle into the back of the car, and she took him home. His mother was on her knees beside the front steps, weeding a flower bed. She looked up with dismay in her eyes. "Not another flat tire, Alec."

"It's okay, Mom. I've got a patch kit."

Ruth sighed. "That tire is going to be almost solid patches before long," she said, but Alec had already vanished around the corner of the house. "Thank you for bringing him home." She stripped off her gloves. "Would you like some coffee?"

Deborah must have looked startled.

Ruth said diffidently, "Coffee sounds sort of silly when it's so warm, doesn't it? But sometimes when the weather is like this, if I drink something hot it makes me feel cooler."

"I'll try it. Thanks."

It was pleasant inside the house, at least in comparison to the rising heat outdoors. There was a whisper of a breeze through the open kitchen windows, where crisp white curtains had been tied back out of the way. Deborah sat down at the small table and wondered if she dared to bring up the subject of Paradise Valley.

She had forgotten to ask Riley whether he had talked to Ruth yet. She suspected he had not, and she also thought that he'd rather forget the whole thing. Well, that was understandable, she supposed; he didn't want to take the chance of infuriating what was obviously a good and sincere employee. But Deborah didn't have that consideration holding her back. And now that she had been offered the chance...

Ruth pushed aside a sketch pad and a box of cheap watercolors and set two ceramic mugs on the table. Deborah picked up hers—Love Is Like a Mushroom, it said on the side, with a sketch of half a dozen toadstools—and sipped her coffee. Then, looking for a way to break the ice, she pointed at the box of watercolors. "I had the impression that Alec never sits still long enough to paint," she said.

"He doesn't," Ruth said a little stiffly. "I do. Just for something to pass the time. The days get long sometimes."

"May I look?" The question sprang automatically to Deborah's lips, and the cover of the sketchbook was open before she realized there had not been an answer.

Ruth's mouth had tightened into a firm line, but all she said was a quiet, "If you like."

When will you learn? Deborah asked herself. *Ruth said it was only a way to pass the time. Of course she doesn't want to show you her work. A lot of people don't.* Others—well, the mere fact that Deborah Ainsley had asked to look had convinced more than one hopeful amateur that she was the next Mary Cassatt, and that was even worse.

Just glance at the drawings, say something noncommittal and get out of here before you have another attack of tactlessness, Deborah ordered herself. *Let Riley deal with the rest. She's his friend, after all, not yours.*

She glanced. Then she set her coffee cup firmly out of the way, pulled the sketchbook closer and looked long and thoroughly at every sheet. At a small blond girl with a jump rope, at a towheaded boy with a cat curled on his shoulders, at a child in a hooded yellow slicker squatting over a rain puddle.

She looked up finally and said sternly, "*This* is just a way to pass your time?"

Ruth colored. "Not exactly," she said.

"Well, I should hope you know better than that. You should be ashamed of yourself for saying it. No wonder you asked about my gallery."

"I thought maybe if I could work up my nerve to ask you to look at my things... But then you said you were going to close it, so..." Ruth reached for the sketchbook almost protectively.

Deborah held it out of her reach and pulled out one of the larger drawings, of a tiny girl sitting at a miniature tea table with her three guests—a teddy bear, a china doll and a small dog wearing a baby's bonnet. "I'd like to buy this," she said.

"I—I've never sold anything," Ruth admitted. "I wouldn't even know how much to ask for it."

"Believe me, I know what it's worth," Deborah said firmly, and told her. "And as for the rest..."

Ruth swallowed hard, but all she said was, "Would you like more coffee?"

"I think you'd better make another pot," Deborah told her. "We've got a lot to talk about."

CHAPTER NINE

IT WAS THE STRANGEST thing Deborah had ever seen, actually watching as years peeled away from a woman's face as she glimpsed a new world opening up before her. But at the same time, she saw a sort of exalted strain come into Ruth's eyes, and finally the woman asked, in little more than a whisper, "What if I can't do it?"

"You're already doing it," Deborah said, and added dryly, "If you have trouble, just pretend you're only painting to pass the time!"

By the time she left a couple of hours later, the agreements were made; it was only a matter of the paperwork. Ruth had announced her intention of signing the contracts the moment they came into her hands.

"I'm gratified, but I'd feel better if you'd have an attorney look everything over first," Deborah told her. She drained her mug and thoughtfully read the rest of the motto, printed coyly on the bottom, where it was nearly always hidden by the contents of the cup. Ruth was right about the coffee, she thought. She did feel cooler after the hot drink.

And the wisdom printed in the mug? Was Ruth right about that, too?

Don't think about it, Deborah told herself. *Just be glad that this trip hasn't been a total washout.* Finding Ruth made it all worthwhile.

Just keep thinking that way, she told herself, *and someday you might make yourself believe it.* Finding Ruth. Finding Riley. There was no comparison.

She considered stopping at the restaurant again, but in the end she drove on past and went back to Lassiter House instead. Riley obviously hadn't been feeling desperate for her company this morning, and she didn't feel up to being rejected again. Besides, it was only fair to let Ruth have the joy of telling Riley, or the alternate fun of holding her good news close to her heart for a while, keeping it secret from the world.

The thought of secrets finally reminded her of Paradise Valley, and the talk she had originally meant to have with Ruth. She sighed. Perhaps it was just as well that she hadn't brought it up, and risked this fledgling partnership that promised so much for Ruth. No matter what happened to the resort, she and Alec wouldn't be destitute as long as Ruth kept painting.

You're beginning to sound cynical, Deborah told herself. *Don't give up yet. Fred Milligan may come through with flying colors. And Aunt Ida may suddenly acquire wisdom, too,* she mocked herself, *and Preston Powell may have a massive attack of conscience and return everyone's money in the town square at high noon, but I wouldn't count on it!*

She knew what was really bothering her, of course, and once back at the house she threw herself down on a chaise longue beside the pool and gave herself a good lecture.

It will pass, she told herself firmly. *This entire infatuation of yours with Riley will go away. It's not surprising that you got caught up in it, but once you're away from him things will get back to normal. You always knew this was only temporary, anyway.*

She sighed and put her hands over her eyes and tried again.

This is the strangest infatuation you've ever heard of, she reminded herself. *How can you possibly be in love with a man you cordially detest half the time?*

But I don't detest him, she corrected herself. *And even though this is certainly not the normal, madly passionate sort of love affair...*

"Don't kid yourself about that, either," she muttered. If what had happened in his apartment on Saturday night wasn't madly passionate, then Deborah Ainsley hadn't any idea what would be. If she was looking for fireworks, well, she had found out on Saturday night that the potential was certainly there.

For a full minute she lost herself in pleasant, dreamy memories of the way he had kissed her and the shivers of pleasure that had racked her body and made her want so much more. And then, finally, she sat up and reminded herself that while Riley had without a doubt shared the pleasure of those sensations, his reaction had been much different. He hadn't been able to get rid of her fast enough. And since then, he'd scarcely touched her at all.

He certainly doesn't find anything about me to be overwhelmingly attractive, she told herself bluntly, *or he wouldn't have turned down that invitation I issued.*

No amount of money would be enough to make me marry you, he had said once. It was painfully obvious, she thought, that he'd considered the question carefully, and found the price unbearable.

It's only infatuation, she told herself firmly. *You can't actually be in love with someone who turns pale at the sight of you!*

She knew, down deep, that infatuation was a bonfire that flared high and then burned out, but she also knew that the feeling she held in her heart for Riley was more like a furnace; not flashy, perhaps, but solid and reliable and always, always there.

And, even if there had ever been a chance of changing that, of backing out of loving him, it was too late to do anything about it now.

Ruth had been right about that, too.

Love Is Like a Mushroom, that silly ceramic mug of hers had proclaimed. You Never Know If It's the Real Thing Until It's Too Late.

WHEN MARY BETH THREW a party, she didn't waste effort on a small one, Deborah found herself thinking that evening. The two private dining rooms that overlooked the river had been opened into one for the event, and Mary Beth's friends filled it to the point of claustrophobia. Deborah suspected that if a third room had been available, Mary Beth could have filled that one, as well. She certainly had no shortage of friends, and she seemed to want Deborah to know them all, too.

It's a microcosm of what my wedding reception would have been like, Deborah thought. With Aunt Ida doing the planning for one half of the family and Mary Beth in charge on the other side, it would have been the biggest party southern Illinois ever saw. Aunt Ida was right; the church probably wouldn't be big enough!

"You're looking pensive," Riley murmured, beside her.

She tried to smile. "I was just thinking that if this wedding actually was taking place, you wouldn't have any choice about finishing your party rooms upstairs. I'm surprised Aunt Ida hasn't questioned you about when you'll be starting and how long it's going to take."

He glanced over his shoulder warily. "Thanks for the warning. I'll keep my distance from her."

"You mean she's here tonight?" Deborah was astounded. "I thought this was a strange collection of people, but I never expected Aunt Ida would be on Mary Beth's list of friends!"

"Calling them all friends is a bit euphemistic, perhaps. The guest list also includes all of Rod's clients," Riley reminded her. "Preston Powell is here, too, for instance. Mary Beth has the politics of a small town laid out like a mathematical equation, and she makes it a practice not to leave out anyone."

"Oh, is that why she's been exhibiting me? I was beginning to feel like a scientific curiosity."

"Don't let it bother you. She's probably just rehearsing the receiving line for the wedding."

"That's such a comfort, Riley." She allowed a hint of sarcasm to creep in; at least it was better than sounding as if she was on the brink of tears.

She turned toward the buffet table, mostly so she didn't have to look up at him and smile convincingly. Ruth, in uniform, was replacing a half-empty pan of Swedish meatballs with one that was heaped full. From the corner of her eye, Deborah thought she saw a look of surprise flash across the woman's face, but an instant later all trace of it was gone, if it had ever been there at all, and Ruth offered her a plate with a conspiratorial smile.

You're seeing things, Deborah told herself.

Her nerves were shot; she admitted it. It was agony enough to stand beside him and play the public part of the adoring fiancée, when she wanted with every fiber of her being for it to be true instead of only a masquerade. But it was even more difficult to play the private role of slightly cynical Deborah, always willing to fence with good old Cousin Riley, when she wanted to fling herself into his arms instead and plead with him to love her.

It was a relief when Riley murmured that he had to check on something in the main dining room, and went away. She didn't see him again for the better part of an hour, and by then she was starting to fret about his absence.

Dammit, Deborah, she finally told herself, *I wish you'd make up your mind!*

That was about the time that she realized the crowd was changing; it was quieter, for one thing, and everybody seemed to have stopped milling about. People were settling into groups, looking expectantly at Mary Beth, who stood near the windows with a small silver dinner bell in her hand.

Please, not party games, Deborah thought. *If she starts something juvenile like musical chairs...*

She did not. Instead Mary Beth called Riley to her side and thanked him, and summoned Deborah to introduce her, as if, Deborah thought, she hadn't already made introductions to everyone already! Then Mary Beth's laugh rang out, just as pleasant as the sound of the bell. "And now that we have the guests of honor up here where they belong," she said, "let's get down to the real intention of this party—the entertainment!" She rang the bell furiously; the double doors across the room were flung open, and Ruth wheeled in a huge serving cart, heaped with boxes and parcels brightly wrapped and ribboned, a loving shower of gifts from good friends to a future bride and groom.

Deborah wanted to groan. She glanced at Riley; he looked just as startled as she felt, but she still wanted to kick him. Mary Beth was *his* sister, after all. He should have suspected what she was capable of doing!

Mary Beth's perfect smile reached almost from ear to ear. "You didn't have a clue, did you?" she said with a chuckle. "I'm so proud of us all. Nobody breathed a single hint!"

That must have been why Ruth looked surprised, Deborah thought. She thought it must have been obvious what was going on, and therefore no surprise at all. But of course Ruth would have known about the cartload of gifts building up outside the door....

She turned on Riley suspiciously. "Wait a minute," she said under her breath. "You told me you were going out to the main dining room. How could you not know about this? You must have seen that pile of packages!"

"I never got outside this room. Rod had some business." He sighed. "Damn. I should have seen this coming."

"That's right. You should have. Now what do we do? Have our final and climactic fight?"

"We open the gifts and say thank-you and smile prettily."

Deborah glared at him. "Just be sure you keep track of which name goes with which gift," she muttered. "Because you are going to get the joy of returning all of them!"

No nightmare could have made her feel as crazily topsy-turvy as that simple bridal shower did. When she opened a box containing a cut-crystal vase, or a handmade pillow, or a set of napkins, she had to swallow hard to keep from imagining its place in the apartment upstairs. She managed to laugh her way through a thank-you for the set of red satin sheets, while her heart shuddered with the pain of thinking of a wedding night that could never be. And she did her best to look modestly coy when Riley—and of course it had to be Riley who opened that particular gift— lifted a black lace negligee from a box, and someone at the back of the room called, "I thought the presents were supposed to be for both of them!"

"Don't worry about it," Riley assured the heckler, with a soulful look at Deborah. "I'm sure I'll enjoy this one just as much as Debbie does." Then, for good measure, he kissed her, a long and soft and lingering caress.

She thought fleetingly about using his own bow tie to strangle him, but before she could make up her mind whether the undoubted satisfaction would be worth it, a movement from the doorway caught her eye, and her father walked in, his silver hair ablaze under the glow of the chandeliers.

"Daddy?" she muttered. "But he's not supposed to be here till tomorrow!"

Riley had obviously seen him, too. "You seem to have failed to tell me that he was coming at all, Deb."

"Well, I'd have remembered to tell you if you hadn't been so short with me this morning." She pushed a big, silver-wrapped package aside and stood up. "Daddy!" she called, and hurried across the room to greet him, stretching up on her toes to kiss his cheek. It was at that instant she realized that the man who had come into the room behind William Ainsley didn't belong there, either. Not tonight, not tomorrow, not at all.

"And you've brought Bristol, too," she said weakly. "How—nice to see you."

Riley had a little more command of himself. He seized Bristol's hand and shook it heartily and at length. Under the cover of his loud and enthusiastic greeting, Deborah whispered, "Daddy, how could you do this to me?"

William shrugged. "He turned up at my office at the foundation this afternoon. He was on his way down here and wanted Ida's address," he said unhappily. "I certainly couldn't stop him from coming, so I decided the best thing to do was come along.''

She glared at him. ''I hope you explained it.''

''Of course I did. But I must say—'' he waved a hand at the table, strewn with wrapping paper and boxes and gifts ''—I didn't expect to have to explain something like this. What the hell is going on, Deborah?''

Despite Riley's best efforts at holding him captive, Bristol had managed to disentangle himself. He looked sternly down at Deborah, but he didn't make a move to kiss her cheek, or even to touch her at all. ''Deborah, where may I find your Aunt Ida? I must speak to her immediately concerning my discoveries.''

''What discoveries?'' Riley said.

Deborah was almost afraid to hope. ''You found something out about Paradise Valley?''

Bristol drew himself up even straighter. ''Deborah, time is critical,'' he reminded. ''Where is your Aunt Ida?''

''Over there—'' She waved a hand toward the windows.

A gravelly voice right behind her said, ''What the devil is going on here? William, must you always poke your nose into things where you aren't wanted? You were invited for tomorrow. And who is this you've brought with you?''

''Oh,'' Deborah said faintly. ''This is Aunt Ida, Bristol.''

Bristol made a stiff little bow. ''Madam,'' he began, ''I am a friend of Deborah's—''

Riley whispered, ''Friend? It looks to me as if he's rubbed you right off his list, Deb.''

She stepped on his toe as hard as she could.

''I've come all the way from San Francisco to talk to you, Miss Lassiter. At first, when Deborah requested me to look into this matter of the Paradise Valley resort—''

"You asked for this, Deborah?" Riley's voice was no longer a whisper. Still, no one more than a couple of feet away could have heard him over the sudden surprised murmur of the crowd.

"I am not interested in discussing—" Ida began.

"Not here, certainly," Riley said hastily. One hand closed firmly on Ida's arm, the other on Bristol's, and he started for the door. "Deb, get the sna—I mean, ask Powell if he'd step out here."

Preston Powell shrugged and followed, with William and Deborah at his heels.

Bristol was still talking. "This kind of scam absolutely shocks and horrifies me. I had no idea such things went on—"

Riley kicked the door shut on the excited murmurs from the party room. The hallway just outside wasn't very big, and it was awfully crowded with all of them pressed in together. But there seemed to be nowhere else to go.

Bristol didn't even have to raise his voice here. Nevertheless, even Ida seemed to realize that there was no stopping him, so she merely glared at him instead as he summarized what he had discovered.

It was apparent, Deborah thought as she listened, that his interest had been piqued by the whole affair. She hadn't seen this much animation in Bristol's face in all the time she'd known him.

Preston Powell leaned against the door of the party room, smiling a little and shaking his head sadly every couple of minutes as he listened.

Finally, Bristol stopped, out of breath, indignation still seeping from every pore.

Ida was frowning. *She looks confused,* Deborah thought. *That's good. Obviously Bristol has shaken her confidence.*

Preston Powell didn't move. "Very interesting," he said. "Very dramatic. Of course, that's all it is—drama. You've got no right to accuse me. I'm a decent, hardworking citizen who has never been convicted of anything. Now I'd like to return to the party, if you please. Ida?"

Deborah's jaw dropped. Could he really be so certain of Ida that he wasn't even going to defend himself? "Aunt Ida, please!" she pleaded, and seized the woman's elbow. "You have to listen to Bristol."

Ida shook her arm free. "No, Deborah, I don't have to. I've already asked my attorney to look into it."

"Rod? Some good that will do! He's so sold on the idea himself that he can't possibly be objective." It was out before she considered what she was saying, and Deborah glanced guiltily over her shoulder, half-afraid that Mary Beth might have followed them into the hall and overheard that tactless comment. Then she reminded herself that it wouldn't have mattered; she wasn't going to be Mary Beth's sister-in-law, anyway.

"No, I don't mean Rod," Ida said very clearly. "Rod's a very pleasant young man, but he isn't experienced in these things. I meant my former attorney. Mr. Milligan still advises me now and then. In fact, he called me just this afternoon."

Deborah almost sagged in relief. *Good old Fred,* she thought. *He came through for me after all!*

"And he's coming down tomorrow to look over the financial records and the...what is it, Preston? Oh, yes, the prospectus, that's what it's called."

Deborah had turned to look at Preston Powell in triumph, and she was watching him as Ida went on.

"I certainly hope that you will all take Mr. Milligan's word for it when he's looked everything over," Ida said. "He's in the fraud division of the state's attorney general's office now, and this is the kind of thing he looks into all the time.''

Preston Powell had turned deathly white, and his Adam's apple bobbed so furiously that Deborah thought it was going to burst.

''Ida—'' His voice was little more than a croak. ''You should have warned—'' He gulped. ''You should have let me know so I could have a presentation ready.''

Ida's forehead wrinkled in concern. ''Did I forget to tell you that Mr. Milligan was coming, Preston? So foolish of me. But then it's been such a busy day, with selling Lassiter House and—''

Even William was part of the outcry on that one. Paradise Valley was momentarily forgotten.

Deborah rolled her eyes and sat down on the nearest radiator. If there were any more shocks in the offing, she didn't think she could trust herself to remain standing up.

Ida held up a hand to her hearing aid. ''Will you all stop?'' she said petulantly. ''It's just a jumble when you all talk at once, and it hurts my ears. Mr. Powell tells me that we need to have a chat, and I'm very tired, so I think we'll be going home now.''

Deborah slid off the radiator. ''Aunt Ida,'' she said desperately, ''don't talk to him!''

Ida's eyebrows soared. ''Why on earth shouldn't I?''

''At least wait till Fred Milligan gets here tomorrow.''

''Oh, do you know Fred, Deborah? He's such a brilliant man, don't you think? I must be going now, dear. Enjoy the rest of your party.''

Deborah was grasping at straws. ''If you insist on doing this, then take Bristol with you,'' she said. ''He can look after your interests, at least.''

''My interests?'' Ida said sternly. ''What on earth do I know about the man, Deborah, except that he very rudely pushed his way into a private party and made some extremely serious charges without evidence to back them up? I don't care to take up the gentleman's time with my interests.''

There seemed to be no answer to that, and before Deborah could even croak, Ida and Preston Powell were gone.

Deborah sagged into Riley's arms. For a long moment, the silence in the hallway was complete. Then Riley cleared his throat and said glumly, "Every human being has a right to be a damn fool.''

"I am sick of hearing you say that,'' she snapped.

Riley looked as startled as if she'd slapped him.

"Never mind,'' she said helplessly. It was scarcely his fault that the phrase had been running through her mind for two days. "What on earth do we do now?''

"Go open the rest of the gifts?''

That didn't even deserve an answer; she simply stared up at him as if he'd grown a second head.

"Sorry,'' he said. "Keep Preston away from the books so he can't make last-minute alterations, I suppose.''

"How? By setting fire to Lassiter House?''

William asked, "Has she really sold it?''

"Probably. What difference does it make?'' Deborah shook her head, trying to clear it, and then remembered that Bristol was watching. She gathered her strength and pushed herself gently away from Riley. He let her go quite easily.

"We could all go up there,'' William offered.

"I doubt it would do any good,'' Deborah said. "I doubt anything would do any good, now. We'll just have to talk to Fred Milligan tomorrow, that's all. Surely with all of us chiming in, he'll have to listen. Thanks for trying, Bristol.''

He nodded stiffly. "There were too many things interfering with my concentration. Next time..."

"Unfortunately, we aren't likely to get a second chance at him," Riley pointed out crisply.

"That's enough, both of you. Daddy, please."

William stepped forward. "Perhaps if we just got out of the way, Bristol."

"Of course." But Bristol stopped a couple of steps away and turned, a frown cutting into his forehead. "I don't understand you at all, Deborah," he said. "To have engaged yourself to this person... Don't you realize that your own children will also be your third cousins once removed? The chance you're taking—"

"Is minimal, so don't let it keep you up nights, Bristol," Riley recommended.

William tugged Bristol off down the hallway. "You and Deborah can talk about it tomorrow," he was saying as they went out of sight.

Deborah put one hand to her head, which felt as if it were about to explode. "He's taking the engagement seriously," she said helplessly.

"Of course he is. I told you even before I met him that the man has no sense of humor. What's it going to be, Debbie darling? Shall we have the rest of the gifts, or are you anxious to have our final and climactic fight, and get it over with?"

"The gifts," she said absently. "I don't have enough energy left for a messy public fight."

He smiled down at her, and his eyes lit to a brilliant hazel glow. "That's my girl," he said.

And Deborah thought, *I only wish I was....*

TUESDAY MORNING dawned with the sky overcast and threatening rain; still, Deborah was awake early, after a restless night in which she had not been able to uncoil her tense body enough even to rest. For all she knew, Ida and Preston Powell were still locked in the study, where they'd been closeted when Riley brought her home well after midnight. It had taken that long to get all those blasted gifts hauled up to his living room.

Finally she put on shorts and a shirt and padded downstairs, barefoot, to seek out a cup of coffee. At least with a dose of caffeine inside her, she'd have an easy excuse for being so jumpy, she reasoned.

She was not surprised to find her father and Bristol already in the dining room, each gloomily scanning a section of the morning newspaper. Her father, still stubbly-faced, was wrapped in his favorite disreputable bathrobe; Bristol, on the other hand, was wearing a charcoal-gray suit with a crisp white shirt and a red tie, as if he were on his way to a major negotiating session. Deborah sat down beside him with her coffee and almost choked on the cloud of after-shave that surrounded him.

"Has Aunt Ida been down?" she said finally.

William shook his head, without raising it from the sports section.

"I suppose that means Preston succeeded in explaining away any niggling doubts we might have given her, and he's gone out to the golf course to celebrate."

"Haven't seen him, either," William said.

"I have to give the man credit," Deborah murmured. "He certainly works hard at his chosen method of making a living."

Bristol merely looked at her.

Riley's right, Deborah thought. *Bristol doesn't have so much as a shred of humor in his whole body. How could I ever have imagined that I might want to live with this rigid framework of a man? He'd have squeezed the joy right out of me.*

Daddy was right, long ago, too, she thought. *It was security I wanted, and so I chose Bristol. But even I knew, down deep inside my heart, that he wasn't right for me. That's why I haven't been in any hurry to marry him. And now that the wounds Morgan left on me have finally healed, I can see that Bristol would be every bit as bad for me. And so,* she thought ironically, *I've decided I want Riley instead. You're an idiot, Deborah Ainsley.*

Riley came down the hall from the kitchen with a cup already in his hand and a bounce in his step. He was wearing cut-off jeans, running shoes and a polo shirt, and he was the only one who looked as if he'd had enough sleep.

That makes sense, Deborah thought. *He's also the only one of us who's a little better off than he was yesterday. He may still be fighting the battle of Paradise Valley, but one of his problems is solved. He's all but rid of me!*

"When are we expecting Fred Milligan?" he asked.

It was Ida who answered him, from the door that led into the main hallway. "He'll be here for lunch. I hope you'll all stay." There was a faint note of irony as she surveyed her four uninvited guests. "Preston sends his regrets, by the way."

"Regrets?" Deborah said blankly. "You mean, he's gone?"

"Yes. He left Lassiter House last night, quite late, after we finished our little talk."

"You kicked him out?" William asked. "Ida, I congratulate you."

Ida looked at him coldly. "I did not evict him, William. He chose to go."

"I'll bet," Deborah said. "And he's probably scooping up the money right now so he can run before Fred Milligan arrives.'' She propped her elbows on the table and stared morosely into her coffee cup.

"I'm quite sure he will avoid meeting Fred," Ida said. "But he's not taking any money, except for the certified check I gave him. I bought his entire interest in Paradise Valley, you see. I own it now—all of it." She looked around at them with a proud smile.

William put his head down on the newspaper. Riley and Deborah uttered a mutual groan. Bristol looked intrigued.

Ida seemed hurt. "It was a very small certified check actually, just enough to get him out of town, and make the transfer legal. And don't worry that he slipped any of the assets out from under my nose, either. I've been keeping a very close eye on them, along with my banker and Fred Milligan and a few other people who had their reasons to want to see Preston Powell taken down a few notches. As a matter of fact, I thought you'd all be pleased. Now we've got Paradise Valley out of the hands of the swindlers who have held it for ten years, and we can do something legitimate. I bought it for five cents on the dollar, and Preston was delighted to sign it over and get out of town before the fraud division showed up."

The silence that fell in the dining room was absolute. It was Riley who finally said, "You knew he was a crook?"

Ida sniffed. "I suppose I should be pleased at how well I obviously played my part. Still, I don't find it flattering that you all believed I was dizzy enough not to see through a scam like that. Especially you, Deborah." She shook her head primly. "To think that you had so little trust in me that you would go to such great lengths in an attempt to protect the Lassiter money!"

"Such lengths?" Deborah repeated. Her voice sounded a little hollow.

"Yes, dear," Ida said gently. "This nonsense of yours about being engaged to Riley."

Deborah, instantly suspicious, turned to stare at her father, but William looked just as awestruck as she was. Then she realized there was a dancing light in Riley's eyes—not a guilty gleam, however, but a dawning glimmer of appreciation. "We've been taken for a ride, Deb," he said.

"Aunt Ida," Deborah said helplessly. "You knew, and you didn't say anything?" It was impossible, she thought, and yet in a crazy way everything fit.

"It was very naughty of me, wasn't it? I didn't catch on at first, you know. I don't mind telling you that I played terrible bridge that first afternoon when you'd just made your announcement. I lost every rubber. But that night at the restaurant it all fell into place. You did a very convincing job, both of you, but it was the only explanation that made sense, you see. You and Riley..." She shook her head. "It was nonsense to think you could be serious about each other."

Right, Deborah thought morosely. *It's nonsense. And if you've got any brains at all, Deborah, you'll remember that.*

"I could hardly take you into my confidence," Ida went on. "You were far too useful in diverting Preston's attention from what I was doing. But I'm afraid I just couldn't resist egging you on a little."

Deborah sighed. "So that's when you started making wedding plans that kept getting wilder by the minute."

Ida looked just a tiny bit guilty. "I simply couldn't resist seeing how far I could go before you would protest. I found myself looking at it in very much the same way I thought about Preston Powell, you see."

"This ought to be good," Riley said under his breath.

Ida smiled at him gently, and said almost apologetically, "One good scam deserves another. And you had both asked for it, you know."

CHAPTER TEN

RILEY GAVE a sudden shout of laughter. "Ida, you're priceless," he said. "But tell me, please, just what you plan to do with that decrepit resort, now that you own it. It's still going to cost a fortune to build hotels and ski ramps, you know."

"Old people like me don't want hotels and ski ramps," Ida said calmly. "They want good, pleasant housing without having to worry about upkeep and maintenance. They want community activities like a clubhouse and a swimming pool and a bingo hall, and they want—"

"You're turning it into a senior citizen complex?"

"Don't worry, Riley," Ida said dryly. "It will work. I've done my research."

He shook his head admiringly. "I don't doubt it for a minute."

"And as a matter of fact, there's a small and quiet waiting list for the apartments and town houses we're going to build in the place of all those summer palaces Preston had planned.

"*We* being you and Fred Milligan?" Deborah speculated.

"And a fair number of other investors, yes. Anyone who wants out will have no trouble selling those pretty stock certificates Preston gave them. Personally, I think they'll make more by staying in, but then sometimes—"

"Venture capital is a risky business," Deborah recited in unison with her. "Tell me one thing, Aunt Ida. If Fred Milligan is in this up to his neck, why was he so suspicious when I called him?"

Ida looked at her as if she were a mildly stupid child. "Of course he was suspicious," she said. "He was sitting in Springfield chewing his nails while I laid the foundations. It's no wonder the poor man was getting nervous waiting for his cue. And then you called up and told him 'Aunt Ida's up to no good' or something of the sort, and he didn't even know which side you were on, for heaven's sake!"

"I'm glad *someone* in your crowd had an anxious moment over this," Deborah said disgustedly.

Bristol cleared his throat. "Since obviously none of this has anything to do with me, I am going back to Chicago. Shall I wait for you, William?" he asked, with a scathing look at the disreputable bathrobe.

"I suppose there's no need for me to stay to talk to the minister now, is there?" William said with a weak smile.

"That's right," Deborah told him coolly.

"Then unless you'd like me to keep you company. . ."

She took pity on him; he was so obviously grasping for an excuse. "Don't worry about Daddy, Bristol. I'll be driving back myself later today." She bit her lip and added, "I'm sorry you had to miss the rest of your seminar for nothing."

He nodded, matter-of-factly accepting the apology. "There will be other seminars. I found the matter quite interesting, actually." He nodded to Ida, and was gone.

Well! Deborah thought. *He doesn't seem to care whether I'm engaged or not!*

The loss of his company did not seem to disturb Ida. He was no more than out the door when she asked, "And the rest of you? Will you be staying to have lunch with Fred?"

"I don't think so, Aunt Ida," Deborah said dryly. "You seem to have everything well under control."

William excused himself to get dressed, and Ida murmured something about needing to get busy because she had wasted far too much time in the past couple of days. She hurried off toward the kitchen.

She's wasted time, Deborah thought. *Studying bridal magazines, I suppose she means, and thinking up all those idiotic twists. How could I have been such a chump?*

She didn't look at Riley. She toyed with her coffee cup instead. "I suppose I should go and pack, too," she said finally.

She knew he was watching her; he was sitting at an angle, one arm stretched over the high back of his chair, his long legs occupying a great deal of the space between her and the door. She thought for a moment that he wasn't going to answer, but finally he said, very quietly, "Deborah..."

She waited, but he didn't go on. Her nerves were stretched as taut as violin strings. She gave Darlene Lassiter's diamond ring a tug and succeeded only in jamming her knuckle. She gritted her teeth and twisted the narrow band on her finger, and finally it slid free, leaving a patch of reddened, abused skin. She held the ring for a single tick of the clock and then dropped it into his hand. "Thanks for the loan," she said. "I don't think I've hurt it." It sounded a little sad, and she tried to recover with a laugh. "We never got to have our final climactic fight, after all."

He smiled, a little. She saw the corner of his mouth quirk, even though she wasn't looking straight at him. "That's just as well, don't you think?"

She nodded. "I suppose so. This way you can just tell everyone we fought it out over the telephone, or something. Whatever you like. It doesn't matter." She bit her lip and looked down at her now bare hand, holding the edge of the table, waiting for him to go.

But he did not leave. Instead, his hand slipped from the back of his chair to the nape of her neck, and pulled her ever so gently toward him. By the time she realized his intention, it was too late; she could not stand up or lean away or even turn her head at all. All she could do was raise a hand and spread it across his chest, directly over the strong beat of his heart. "Please," she whispered, and he let her go.

Instantly, she regretted stopping him. Surely there would have been nothing so very wrong with allowing him to kiss her goodbye. She could have had one last warm, strong caress to tuck into her heart. But it was safer this way, she knew, for probably it would not have been the lover's kiss she craved, but a cousin's, and that would have been a memory to haunt her.

She walked with him to the front door, silently. On the terrace, in the brilliant sunshine that had burned away the morning's dull grayness, he said, "See you around, kid."

"Of course," she said, trying to sound casual. "We're family. Call me next time you come to Chicago."

"I'll do that." He flicked a careless finger across her cheek and down the line of her jaw. Then he was gone.

At the bottom of the hill, he stopped and turned, and automatically she raised an arm to wave to him. Her chest seemed to constrict, and her breath came in gasps. *If I call to him,* she thought, *will he hear me? Will he come back? Is he having second thoughts about leaving me?*

But it was not at her that he was looking, and he did not see her wave. Someone else had hailed him, then came down the street and dropped into step with him—a small figure with white-gold hair. Alec, she thought, and her arm dropped to her side as if the muscles had been cut. The man and the boy went out of sight beneath the trees, absorbed in conversation. Whatever they were talking about, Deborah knew, she had no part in it. She had already been forgotten.

She went back into Lassiter House and up the stairs to the guest room to pack her bags.

CHICAGO'S MAGNIFICENT Mile—the mad bustle of pedestrians surging in waves down the sidewalks, the constant roar of traffic on North Michigan Avenue, the distant wail of a dozen sirens scurrying in all directions. Once not so very long ago the city's busy roar had been Deborah's lifeblood. Now the packs of pedestrians gave her claustrophobia, and the noxious fumes of the cars and buses choked her, and the sirens made her head ache.

The Ainsley Gallery was quiet and peaceful, still a haven for the art lover, though it no longer was for the owner. She was honest enough to admit, however, that it was not the gallery, or the city that had changed; it was Deborah herself. And she knew that with one small change, she could again be very happy here. One very small addition, really, she thought. All it would take was six feet of masculinity, with rumpled reddish-brown hair and a dancing smile.

When the discreet doorbell sounded, Deborah stopped contemplating the calendar spread open on her desk—it had been a mere three weeks since she came back from Summerset, not the six months it seemed—and went out to greet the client who had just come in. Her first glimpse of him brought a tiny smile to her face. "Hi, Daddy," she said. "Happy birthday."

William Ainsley straightened from his inspection of a pastel sketch of a sailboat on Lake Michigan. "Don't remind me," he said with mock grumpiness. Then he pointed at the pastel. "Tell me about the artist."

Deborah glanced at it, and frowned. "I can't," she said, a bit puzzled. "I've never seen that piece before."

Peggy had just come out of the stockroom at the back of the gallery, wrestling with a large flat box. "Actually Deborah," she began hesitantly, "I took that on consignment while you were gone, and..."

Deborah gave her a long, thoughtful stare.

"The papers are on your desk," Peggy offered.

"It's beautiful," Deborah said. *It's a good thing someone's minding the gallery,* she thought. *I haven't been doing a very attentive job of it.*

Peggy's face lit. "I was afraid..." She stopped, as if thinking better of it. "This box just came for you. It's from Summerset."

From Summerset. For an instant Deborah's heart soared, and then she crashed back into reality. *What was I hoping for, anyway?* she asked herself cynically. *A raspberry puff pastry, fresh from Riley's own hands?*

The box was from Ruth Chastain instead, and it was heavy. Deborah carried it back to her office and opened it with a feeling of foreboding; three weeks wasn't much time for the woman to have produced this volume of work, and if it turned out to be less than good...

"I suppose you'll still accept my check," William said, following her into the office.

"With the proper identification," Deborah teased. She looked over her shoulder at Peggy, still in the gallery taking down the pastel. "Did you buy the sailboat? Daddy, you're addicted."

He shrugged. "A birthday gift to myself. What have you got there?" He looked at the top watercolor—a little boy running down the street with his dog—with a reverent whistle. "That's superb. You've got enough there for a show, haven't you?"

"Yes," Deborah said thoughtfully. "I need to talk to Ruth about that, soon. I'm glad you like it. I've got one of her paintings set aside for you, for your birthday. Shall I take you out to dinner tonight and present it?"

"Oh." He sounded ill-at-ease. "I'm sorry, darling. I've already made plans. We're going to the Art Institute to see the new architecture show, but if you'd like to come along, I'm sure Peggy wouldn't mind."

Peggy? It should have been a surprise, but somehow it wasn't. William had been dropping into the gallery more often lately, and now that Deborah stopped to think about it, he and Peggy had seemed to get along rather well.

"I get lonely," he confessed softly. "Deborah, it's not as if I want her to take your mother's place, but—"

Deborah smiled. "Mother would," she said softly. "She'd be cheering you on."

William colored a little. "I am sorry about not thinking of you, though," he said. "I just assumed... but you're not seeing as much of Bristol lately, are you?"

"I'm not seeing him at all," Deborah said crisply. "When he finally realized that I really had gotten myself into a completely fake engagement, he seemed to think I was incredibly loose, or perhaps just a fool, or an adventurer of the worst description.... I'm not sure what he believed—he couldn't seem to make up his mind. I must admit I didn't try very hard to convince him otherwise."

"I'm glad," William said simply. "He was never right for you."

"I only wonder why I couldn't see that," Deborah murmured.

But she knew, and long after her father had gone back to the foundation and the morning edged on toward noon, she was still thinking about it. Bristol's solid reliability had been just what she was looking for after those tumultuous months with Morgan. He had filled a gap in her life, and he had helped her to heal. Then that very same solid reliability threatened to choke her.

There has to be a happy middle ground, she thought. *I want to know where I'm going, yes, but not if the price is having to give up all flexibility about how to get there. I want a certain amount of material comfort, but not at the cost of giving up my peace of mind. I want stability, but not if I have to give up the freedom to laugh at the world.*

I want Riley, that's the bottom line, she admitted. *And it hurts worse than any ache I have ever experienced to know that I cannot have him.*

It was not getting better; three weeks without him had not made the desires fade. *And three years won't, either,* she told herself firmly, *so you might just as well get down to work. You've got a great deal to do here.*

She picked up the watercolor of the little boy and the dog. William was right; when all the paintings were framed and ready to hang, there would be enough for a show, and it would be time to introduce Ruth Chastain to the public. The trick, it was becoming apparent, was not going to be in getting Ruth to work to her capacity, but in properly marketing her, and in convincing her to promote herself. Deborah could already predict the answer if she was to call Ruth and ask her to come to Chicago for a show. The woman would have all kinds of excuses. It would be much easier to deal with Ruth's fear and her lack of self-confidence if they were face-to-face.

But the only way to do that just now was for Deborah to go back to Summerset. And that would probably mean that she would have to face Riley.

But wasn't that inevitable, whether she ever set foot in Summerset again? she asked herself. Sooner or later, Riley was bound to come back to Chicago. He would call her; she had, after all, invited him to do that. Or, worse, he might simply drop in at the gallery unannounced. It would be the cousinly thing to do, after all.

And when that day comes, she told herself, *you'll have to be polite and friendly and casual, without warning and without a chance to practice your family-reunion smile in your mirror. Wouldn't it be better to get it over with on your own terms? It will get easier after the first time.*

She sat at her desk for a long time and thought about it. Then she pushed all the unfinished business into the top drawer, went back to her apartment and packed an overnight bag, and started out for Summerset.

SHE ALMOST TURNED back a half dozen times on the long drive, and even at the front entrance of the restaurant she nearly seized the Jaguar's keys back from the parking valet's hand.

Don't be ridiculous, she lectured herself. *You're here to see Ruth, remember? Anyone—* she paused and rephrased it sternly—*anything else is incidental.*

She squared her shoulders and went in. The blond hostess was nowhere to be seen; Riley himself was in the foyer, studying the delicate drawing of a trumpet vine with what looked like scholarly contemplation. He turned to greet her with a professional smile that froze when he saw her.

Her heart seemed to settle down against her diaphragm with a thud. *That,* she thought, *is not how I would have looked at him if he had walked unexpectedly through the door of the gallery. My reaction would have been much warmer, and ever so much more embarrassing.*

Riley had recovered himself. "This is a surprise."

And not a particularly pleasant one, he seemed to imply. "I'm here on business." Her voice was huskier than she would have liked, but he didn't seem to notice. Why should he, after all? "Not business with you," she added too hastily.

"Of course not." There was an edge of ice in his voice.

"I'm sorry. I didn't mean it to sound that way. I came in to have dinner, actually."

For a moment she thought he was going to throw her out bodily, if only he could bear to bring himself to touch her. Then he reached for a leather-covered menu from the stack and asked quietly, "Will you be alone?"

Unless you'll join me . . . Despite it all, the invitation hovered on her lips. Finally sanity returned and she said, "Yes, I'll be alone. I'd like to have Ruth as my waitress if I could."

He had turned to lead her into the dining room, but he stopped abruptly in the doorway. Deborah, who had closed her eyes momentarily in an effort to keep the tears from forming, bumped into him and had to grab for his arm to steady herself. The scent of him, clean and fresh and masculine, tugged at her senses, and she gritted her teeth against the pain that slashed through her.

"She's not here tonight," Riley said. "She's taking a week off to paint her house."

"Her house?" Deborah said blankly.

There was a brief pause. "She said she was painting. So I assumed . . . But if you're here to see her on business, I gather she's not redecorating her living room, after all."

Deborah tried to laugh. "She'd better not be."

He looked down at her for a full minute. Finally, Deborah realized that her hand was still braced against his arm.

She withdrew it hastily. "I don't think I'll come in after all."

He put the menu back. "As you wish." It was formal, polite.

There was nothing more to say. She started down the slightly angled ramp to the main entrance. She glanced back when she reached the door, cursing her own foolishness even as she did it—if he was watching her, it would only be to make certain she was gone. But he had already retreated to the dining room.

She glanced at the outer door, and then at the dark flight of stairs, and before she realized that she had made a decision, she found herself on the dimly lit landing just outside his apartment, almost out of breath, hoping that the sound of her feet on the stair treads had not echoed down throughout the building.

Downstairs, the massive main door closed with a thud. *If anyone looks up, they'll see me,* she thought, and she twisted the knob and slid into Riley's apartment with a sense of relief that lasted just over three seconds.

Then she leaned against the door and said under her breath, "You fool. Just how do you think you're going to creep back downstairs, with people coming and going all the time?"

Why had she come up here, anyway? Certainly it wasn't because she was embarrassed at having to ask the valet to return a car he had parked just moments ago!

She leaned her head against the door and sighed. She knew, of course, what had brought her here. With Riley fully occupied in the restaurant, she could sneak into his house for just a moment. It would be the last time she would ever step inside these four walls. She could stand here and feel his presence; she could soak up the quiet atmosphere. And perhaps she could begin to let go of the memories.

She pushed herself away from the door and walked cautiously across the room. The only light was the dim glow of street lamps reflected from far below. The only sound was the hum of the mechanical system. The building was too big and too well built for the laughter and conversation from the restaurant to find its way up here.

The apartment was quiet; it was full of his presence. But it was not peaceful—not for her. The feelings that she had hoped would lessen were not only still here, as if trapped in the very air of the room, but they seemed to have grown stronger with a few weeks' absence—the memories of his firm strength as he had held her, of the tender experiment of their first kiss, of how much she had wanted him to make love to her on that last night . . .

The sound of the doorknob turning froze her to the floor in the shadows, and she braced herself for the sudden flooding of light, and the questions, perhaps the accusations, that would follow.

But the light didn't come. The door closed, and Riley crossed the room in darkness, his step sure and firm as if he knew every square inch of the floor. An overstuffed chair yielded a tiny squawk of protest as he dropped into it, his hand over his eyes.

Deborah had to stifle a sudden, hysterical giggle. *It's become a Laurel and Hardy skit,* she thought frantically. *Or a scene out of a situation comedy. What am I supposed to do now? Drop to my knees and crawl frantically for the door?*

"I wish I knew what you were thinking." It was quiet, as if he was talking more to himself than to her. For an instant she was absolutely still; Riley's hand moved to the lamp beside his chair, and a pool of golden light sprang into life.

"How did you know I was here?" she parried.

"You make a lovely silhouette against the windows."

She gathered her dignity. "I shouldn't have trespassed. I'm sorry, Riley."

"Why did you come back here, anyway? Is there something you think you left undone? Or were you just playing Miss Manners and checking to be certain I'd returned all those gifts? Oh, I've got it—the engagement party wasn't enough of a practical joke, so you sneaked in and filled my bathtub with strawberry gelatin, right?"

She cringed at the harshness, for she could not understand his anger. "Riley, please..." she whispered.

"When you came in tonight, I thought..." He broke off and leaped up from his chair to pace across to the windows. "Why the hell did you come here, Deborah?" he asked sharply. "Ruth has a telephone. You know where she lives. If you hate the sight of me so much, why did you bother to come here at all?"

"Hate?" The denial came automatically. "I don't hate the sight of you."

"You seemed to think I was going to drag you back to the kitchen and use you to sharpen knives! You couldn't get out of the restaurant fast enough, and yet I find you up here. Why did you run up here?" he asked. "Aren't you afraid of what I might do?"

She shook her head. "Of course not. You don't have it in you to be violent, Riley. How did you know I was here, anyway? You did know, or you wouldn't have come upstairs at all."

"The valet said you hadn't come outside."

He had followed her, she thought blankly. But he had gone back into the dining room.

"That left this as the only place you could have gone. Does that frighten you even more, to know that I would have chased you down the street?"

"No," she whispered. "But why did you change your mind?"

He sighed heavily. "Because I couldn't let you go like that. Afraid of me."

Something was quivering deep inside her, a newborn hope so fragile that she was afraid to move, afraid to breathe, for fear of crushing it. "What did you mean..." She hardly recognized her own voice because the force of the blood pounding in her ears distorted it so. "Riley, what *did* you think tonight, when I came in?"

For a moment she believed he wasn't going to answer. He stared out the window, one hand braced against the glass. "I thought you might have come because you wanted to see me," he said in a voice so low that she almost couldn't hear. "Because...maybe...you missed me."

Her heart was skittering at such a rate that she couldn't get her breath. "I came because there is something here I want." She steadied her voice as best she could. "You."

He scowled. "That's not funny, Deborah."

"I didn't say it was." She moved very cautiously across the room until she stood behind the overstuffed couch; her fingers dug gratefully into the softly upholstered back, helping to take the strain off her shaking knees. "The practical joke turned itself inside out, Riley. I got caught in it. I fell in love."

She saw something flare in his eyes, something that looked liked fear, and it sent chills through her. *My God,* she thought, *have I gone too far? Telling him I love him? I should not have said that, not yet.*

No, she told herself. *There is no room now for anything but the truth. No matter how badly it hurts, and no mat-*

ter how it ends, there is no other way. I have to know, that's all. And if the answer is the worst, then I'll have to deal with that. But at least I'll know....

"I love you," she said quietly. "I'm sorry if you don't want to hear that, but it's true. And I just need to know if there's a place for me in your life. I don't know what you wanted to say to me downstairs...."

"Don't you?" There was something in his voice that was almost a tremor.

She looked down at her hands, and she didn't see him moving quietly toward her. "But if you missed me, too, and if you want me, I'll stay."

He was at her side. "I did. And I do."

The words almost echoed in the still room, and she wondered if he realized how very much like a vow they sounded. It hurt to know how desperately she wanted him to mean just that, and so she said, quickly and uncomfortably, "It doesn't have to be permanent, Riley."

"Yes, it does." It was uncompromising, as firm as his arms around her. "Very permanent," he said. "Just you and me, Deb."

She released a long, shivery breath, and his mouth came down against hers with an almost hungry urgency, as if he was seeking solace for a soul-deep pain. And since she could not answer him with words, she pressed herself against him and tried to tell him with her body how very glad she would be.

"You'll marry me," he said against the corner of her mouth.

She blinked slowly, and tried to pull herself out of the pleasant fog he had so skillfully induced. "You said there wasn't enough money in the world to make you marry me," she reminded.

He smiled down into her eyes. "I changed my mind," he said gently, and began to kiss her again, concentrating this time on the tender skin of her temple.

The blunt statement jolted her. When he said that, she remembered, it had looked as if her trust fund was going to vanish without a trace. But now that the money was safe—did it make a difference? Was that why he wanted permanence, with a marriage license to ensure it?

She twisted uncomfortably in his arms, and he stopped kissing her. "A dowry is such a civilized custom," he murmured.

She pulled away from him. Misery was starting to rise in a wave, threatening to choke her.

Riley sat down on the couch and tugged her onto his lap. "Debbie, you little fool!" he said fiercely into her ear. "What I said was, no amount of money was enough to make me marry you."

"Isn't that the same thing?" she said uncertainly.

"Not at all." He captured a glossy brown curl and began to wrap it slowly around his finger, drawing her face nearer to his with each revolution. "How much cash have you got in your pockets?"

"What's it to you? About ten dollars, I suppose."

He raised one eyebrow. "It's mere curiosity, but how were you planning to pay for your dinner?"

She said stiffly, "I have a credit card. I left home in a hurry." She stopped abruptly.

He smiled a little. "I see."

She thought, vengefully, that all of a sudden he was seeing a great deal too much. He saw, for instance, that no matter what his reasons, she was too deeply in love to care.

"In any case," he said cheerfully, "ten dollars is plenty. I'll marry you for it. And if you only had two cents, that would be enough, too."

Her nose was almost against his. "Oh," she said softly. "You mean that no amount of money—"

"Would make me marry you. Because money has nothing to do with it. Now will you marry me? Or do you have some general distaste for the state of matrimony that we need to deal with first?"

She would have answered him. But it was impossible to talk when she was being kissed with such skill, and such zeal. And in any case, she thought he probably already knew what she would have said.

It was a long time later that she recovered the power of speech. She was sitting beside him by then, with her head nestled against his shoulder and his arm around her. He was toying with her hair as if he still couldn't quite make himself believe that she was real.

"What if I hadn't come back?" she said finally.

"Well, I wasn't dim enough to sit back and wait for Ida's funeral—that's assuming she has one someday—in the hope that you'd show up to pay your respects. In fact, if you'd like to look at the reservations calendar downstairs you'll see that I've reserved myself all of next week to spend in Chicago."

"Really?"

"Yes. I was hoping that you'd had a chance to miss me, and I was going to do some serious stalking."

She sighed. "I missed you, all right. I'd probably have thrown myself into your arms the minute you showed up."

"Hmm. Perhaps in that case you should have waited for me. It would have been much tidier than this method." But the way he smiled at her made her heart turn over.

"When did you know?" she asked softly.

"That you were going to be the bane of my life again, in a different sort of way?"

She wrinkled her nose at him.

"Sorry," Riley said quickly. "I meant to say, when did I fall in love with you? At breakfast that first morning, I think. I'm absolutely certain I was past saving by dinner that night. The very idea of Bristol Wellington the fifth set my teeth on edge." He drew them along her index finger, as if to prove the point. "And then when you came up with the engagement scheme—"

She sighed. "Not the most brilliant thing I've ever done."

"Oh, I don't know about that. My life just sort of flashed in front of my eyes at that moment."

"You said you didn't want a fiancée," she reminded.

He smiled at her lovingly, and kissed the tip of her nose. "Not a fake one, that's for certain."

"So when you said you had dreams about me in a wedding gown and veil, and things like that—"

"Not a gown," he pointed out. "It was just a veil—and nothing else."

That sent shivers of pleasure up her spine. "Talking of wedding gowns reminds me," she said reluctantly. "We should call Aunt Ida. She's probably already heard from the grapevine that I'm in town."

"Does that mean you're not staying with her?"

Deborah said carefully, "I haven't arranged to do that, no."

He smiled very slowly. "I see. Well, let's not bother her tonight. She'd only start on wedding plans again." He began to nibble at her ear.

"We could elope," she said on a tiny breathless gasp.

"No... we'd better give the party ourselves, or Mary Beth will surprise us with one, and I don't think I could take another one of those." He picked up her hand. "I'm sorry, darling, but I don't have your ring yet. I was going to buy it in Chicago. Only a masochist buys a diamond ring in a town the size of Summerset unless he's quite sure of the answer he's going to get."

She had to smile at that, but she said, "A new ring? I'd much rather have your grandmother's diamond back."

"Are you certain?" It was softly surprised. "But it looked awfully tiny. I'd like to put a whopping big diamond here." He stroked the base of her finger.

She nodded firmly. "I'm certain."

"All right. I'll have the band resized tomorrow, but in the meantime, at least you can look at it." He dug the old velvet box out of his pocket.

"You've been carrying it?"

He admitted unsteadily, "It seemed to bring you closer, somehow."

She snuggled against him, took the ring out of the box and turned it under the light, watching the stone. In the lamplight the diamond seemed brighter, even perhaps more lively, than it had been before. As if it, too, was happy.

The light caught on the engraving inside the band. She tipped it so she could see better, and almost dropped the ring. "Riley, it's our initials!"

He shook his head. "You never looked at it before?"

"I couldn't get it off, remember? It's right there: *D.A. and R.L.*"

"Her name was Darlene Anderson—his was Roger Lassiter."

"It's perfect," she whispered. "And it also says *Forever Yours.*"

"Remember that," he said, and gathered her close again. "Because this is forever ours, Debbie darling. We're all finished with temporary measures."

HARLEQUIN
Romance

A Christmas tradition . . .

Imagine spending Christmas in New
Orleans with a blind stranger and his aged
guide dog—when you're supposed to be
there on your honeymoon!
#3163 Every Kind of Heaven
by Bethany Campbell

Imagine spending Christmas with a man
you once "married"—in a mock ceremony
at the age of eight!
#3166 The Forgetful Bride
by Debbie Macomber

*Available in December 1991, wherever
Harlequin books are sold.*

RXM

"INDULGE A LITTLE" SWEEPSTAKES

HERE'S HOW THE SWEEPSTAKES WORKS

NO PURCHASE NECESSARY

To enter each drawing, complete the appropriate Official Entry Form or a 3" by 5" index card by hand-printing your name, address and phone number and the trip destination that the entry is being submitted for (i.e., Walt Disney World Vacation Drawing, etc.) and mailing it to: Indulge '91 Subscribers-Only Sweepstakes, P.O. Box 1397, Buffalo, New York 14269-1397.

No responsibility is assumed for lost, late or misdirected mail. Entries must be sent separately with first class postage affixed, and be received by: 9/30/91 for the Walt Disney World Vacation Drawing, 10/31/91 for the Alaskan Cruise Drawing and 11/30/91 for the Hawaiian Vacation Drawing. Sweepstakes is open to residents of the U.S. and Canada, 21 years of age or older as of 11/7/91.

For complete rules, send a self-addressed, stamped (WA residents need not affix return postage) envelope to: Indulge '91 Subscribers-Only Sweepstakes Rules, P.O. Box 4005, Blair, NE 68009.

DIR-RL

"INDULGE A LITTLE" SWEEPSTAKES

HERE'S HOW THE SWEEPSTAKES WORKS

NO PURCHASE NECESSARY

To enter each drawing, complete the appropriate Official Entry Form or a 3" by 5" index card by hand-printing your name, address and phone number and the trip destination that the entry is being submitted for (i.e., Walt Disney World Vacation Drawing, etc.) and mailing it to: Indulge '91 Subscribers-Only Sweepstakes, P.O. Box 1397, Buffalo, New York 14269-1397.

No responsibility is assumed for lost, late or misdirected mail. Entries must be sent separately with first class postage affixed, and be received by: 9/30/91 for the Walt Disney World Vacation Drawing, 10/31/91 for the Alaskan Cruise Drawing and 11/30/91 for the Hawaiian Vacation Drawing. Sweepstakes is open to residents of the U.S. and Canada, 21 years of age or older as of 11/7/91.

For complete rules, send a self-addressed, stamped (WA residents need not affix return postage) envelope to: Indulge '91 Subscribers-Only Sweepstakes Rules, P.O. Box 4005, Blair, NE 68009.

© 1991 HARLEQUIN ENTERPRISES LTD.

DIR-RL

INDULGE A LITTLE—WIN A LOT!

Summer of '91 Subscribers-Only Sweepstakes

OFFICIAL ENTRY FORM

This entry must be received by: Oct. 31, 1991
This month's winner will be notified by: Nov. 7, 1991
Trip must be taken between: May 27, 1992—Sept. 9, 1992
(depending on sailing schedule)

YES, I want to win the Alaska Cruise vacation for two. I understand the prize includes round-trip airfare, one-week cruise including private cabin, all meals and pocket money as revealed on the "wallet" scratch-off card.

Name _____

Address _____ Apt. _____

City _____

State/Prov. _____ Zip/Postal Code _____

Daytime phone number _____
(Area Code)

Return entries with invoice in envelope provided. Each book in this shipment has two entry coupons—and the more coupons you enter, the better your chances of winning!

© 1991 HARLEQUIN ENTERPRISES LTD.   2N-CPS

INDULGE A LITTLE—WIN A LOT!

Summer of '91 Subscribers-Only Sweepstakes

OFFICIAL ENTRY FORM

This entry must be received by: Oct. 31, 1991
This month's winner will be notified by: Nov. 7, 1991
Trip must be taken between: May 27, 1992—Sept. 9, 1992
(depending on sailing schedule)

YES, I want to win the Alaska Cruise vacation for two. I understand the prize includes round-trip airfare, one-week cruise including private cabin, all meals and pocket money as revealed on the "wallet" scratch-off card.

Name _____

Address _____ Apt. _____

City _____

State/Prov. _____ Zip/Postal Code _____

Daytime phone number _____
(Area Code)

Return entries with invoice in envelope provided. Each book in this shipment has two entry coupons—and the more coupons you enter, the better your chances of winning!

© 1991 HARLEQUIN ENTERPRISES LTD.   2N-CPS